CHANCE FORTUNE

in the
Shadow
Zone

Chance Fortune and the Outlaws

CHANCE FORTUNE
in the Shadow Zone

SHANE BERRYHILL

A Tom Doherty Associates Book | New York

STARSCAPE

CHANCE FORTUNE IN THE SHADOW ZONE

A Starscape Book
Published by Tom Doherty Associates, LLC
175 Fifth Avenue
New York, NY 10010

www.tor-forge.com

ISBN-13: 978-0-7653-1469-7
ISBN-10: 0-7653-1469-X

First Edition: November 2008

Printed in the United States of America

0 9 8 7 6 5 4 3 2 1

For Sassy

"Behold the stairways which stand in darkness;
behold the rooms of ruin."

—STEPHEN KING,
The Wastelands

ooo

"The mistakes of superheroes
involve too many of us in disaster."

—FRANK HERBERT

ooo

"This little light of mine, I'm gonna let it shine!"

—OLD SPIRITUAL HYMN

CHANCE FORTUNE
in the
Shadow
Zone

1

Chance Fortune and his battle teammates, The Outlaws, stood in an alien dimension beneath an ever-darkening sky. There were no Team Combat Training safeguards to protect them, or any adults, superhuman or otherwise, to rescue them. Only in their teens, The Outlaws had already faced threats most never experience in a lifetime. But all that was nothing in comparison to the challenges that lay ahead of them.

How did this happen? Chance thought. *One minute we were teleporting home from Burlington Academy for the Superhuman. The next, we reintegrated here in the Shadow Zone!*

Chance turned to face Psy-chick, the team's psionic. She looked frightened.

Psy-chick? he thought at her.

She gave no response. Chance guessed fear was preventing Psy-chick from focusing her telepathic powers. His heart went out to her. The two of them had become especially close during their semester together at Burlington.

Chance looked to the rest of his teammates. They all stood peering up at the short, rocky cliffs surrounding them. Hissing and growling echoed from above. Chance saw shadows scurrying about the cliff tops.

Whoever's up there, Chance thought, *they're not friendly! And they've got the high ground. We've got to move before they attack.*

"Guys!" Chance called.

His teammates didn't notice. They stood in a huddle for protection as they gazed upward.

"Shocker!" Chance said. "Get hold of yourself!"

"Too much," Shocker said. He was dressed in his usual attire of leather jacket, jeans, sunglasses, and bandanna. He was crouched on his haunches, scowling with pain as he pressed his hands against his ears. "Too much! It hurts!"

Good lord, Chance thought. *What's gotten into him? No matter. I'll get the others under control first and then deal with it.*

"Snap out of it, you guys!" Chance yelled.

One by one, they did. The Norse demigoddess Iron Maiden rose to stand her full and considerable height. She crossed her well-toned arms over her costume's breastplate.

"Just tell me who to punch, Chance," Iron Maiden said.

The communicator watch riding on Private Justice's lanky, red-and-blue-clad arm produced a hologram of a small, open manual. "The Burlington handbook says one is to always remain calm and call for instructions when faced with a new and potentially dangerous situation."

"Not now, PJ," Chance said. "We need to—"

"Burlington Academy," Private Justice said into his watch, "this is Private Justice of the Outlaws. There has been a malfunction with the teleporter. We didn't make it home. We're trapped in the Shadow Zone! Please respond."

The sound of white noise was the watch's only reply.

"I'll try, Chance," Space Cadet said. The team's technomancer was clad in overstretched purple and white spandex. He adjusted the glasses that sat on his chubby, brown cheeks and began to speak into his watch.

"Burlington, this is Space Cadet. Do you read me, over?" More white noise. "Burlington, this is SC, do you copy, over?" SC looked up and shook his head in confusion. "It's no good, Chance. I . . . I can't make it work."

"It's happened to you, too, hasn't it?" Gothika asked. Days before their departure from Burlington, the Outlaws' witch had used her magic to grow her hair out and highlight its natural ebony sheen with streaks of pink and purple. She maintained the color scheme throughout her outfit. "Chance, something is wrong!"

"Yeah," Chance said. "No kidding."

"No, really!" Gothika said. "I can't *feel*. My sixth sense is gone!"

"What are you saying?" Private Justice asked as he scratched his buzz-cut head.

"My magic," Gothika said. "It's not working!" Gothika hugged herself and began to mumble. "*So hollow. So empty.*"

"And I've gone deaf!" Psy-chick blurted, her voice finding

courage at last. She was dressed in form-fitting black. The white starburst that was her emblem rode on her chest.

"If you've lost your hearing, how do you know what we've been saying?" Iron Maiden asked.

"No, not *deaf deaf!*" Psy-chick said. "I can't hear your thoughts." Psy-chick turned to face Chance, apprehension in her eyes. "Or anyone else's."

"And I can't stretch!" PJ said as he repeatedly thrust out his arms before him.

"What's going on, here?" Iron Maiden asked as she walked toward Chance. "Chance, tell us what's going—*ow!*" Iron Maiden tripped and fell, banging her elbow as she landed. She sat up and massaged her funny bone, her eyes wide with fear. "That *hurt.*"

"But you don't get hurt, Maiden," Psy-chick said.

"Her powers are gone, too!" Gothika said.

"Nonsense!" Iron Maiden said as she shook off her pain and got to her feet. "Here, I'll show you!"

Iron Maiden tried to lift Gothika over her head in a display of superhuman strength. But no matter how much Iron Maiden pulled and tugged, Gothika didn't budge.

Chance reached beneath his black, Zorro-style mask and massaged either side of his nose. They've all lost their powers. Probably even Shocker, though it wouldn't matter one way or another in his current state. This is definitely not good.

The irony of his thoughts was not lost on Chance. He was a normal human and therefore superpowerless to begin with. It had taken a little white lie in that regard to get Chance into Burlington, backed by years of training and study to make the lie stick.

Chance knew if his normalcy ever became known, it would mean immediate expulsion from the school. Never mind that under his leadership the Outlaws had almost won the Team Combat Championship and saved the school from an alien invasion during their first semester. As Private Justice would've said, *the rules were the rules.*

So Chance had never told anyone he was merely human. Not even his closest friends, the Outlaws.

A shrill scream echoed down between the cliffs and the Outlaws jumped with fear. Chance dragged Shocker to his feet.

"Let's move! On me!" He sprinted for the end of the canyon no more than fifty yards away, his teammates obediently following. But it was too late.

2

"Incoming!" Iron Maiden yelled.

The Outlaws were dive-bombed by a human-sized bat. Or rather, it was a human with a bat's face and wings. The Outlaws scattered and rolled.

"No," Chance said. "Don't let them separate us!" Chance felt someone or something clamp its hands around his shoulders. Before he could react, a foot was in the small of his back. Opposing pressure at both points on his body was applied and he flipped head over heels. He impacted the earth hard, churning up black dust and gravel. He spat and coughed.

That's the last time somebody gets the drop on me today! Chance thought as he slammed his fist against the ground.

He looked up to see a small hooded and cloaked figure armed with a bo staff, undoubtedly the one who'd flipped him, making short work of his teammates.

Chance leaped to his feet and sprinted toward the battle,

unsheathing and extending his billy clubs as he ran. He swerved just in time to dodge a blow from an enormous hunchbacked creature wearing a cloak similar to that of the bo staff fighter. He had appeared out of nowhere.

Chance dodged a second blow that shook the ground where it impacted. Chance ran up the length of the hunchback's massive arm and somersaulted off his cloaked shoulders, pelting the attacker across his head while in midflip.

"Ow!" the hunchback cried as he massaged his head. "You no play fair with Brutus!"

"You'll have to pardon me," Chance said as he whirled out of Brutus's path, "if being attacked makes me a bad sport!"

Brutus missed Chance and charged headfirst into the canyon wall. Cracks spiderwebbed from the point of impact. Brutus dropped onto his rear, his eyes rolling in his head. Chance turned and ran toward the small cloaked figure just as the attacker sent the last of the Outlaws tumbling to the ground.

Chance reached him and began throwing the best kicks and swipes he had to offer. His mysterious opponent used the bo staff to expertly block and parry every blow. Chance could not believe his opponent's skill level. He was even better than Anime, Burlington Academy's premiere student martial artist.

Good as he was, the cloaked fighter was not perfect. He ducked under one of Chance's blows a little too late to keep the Outlaw's club from snagging his hood. The weapon's momentum inadvertently yanked the hood off his opponent's head.

Chance froze, stunned at what he saw.

"You're a girl!"

The fighter was a girl about Chance's age, though her hard eyes and sharp features made her seem older. Her head was completely bald and pointy, elfish ears bookended her face. But her most striking feature was her iridescent blue skin.

The girl jerked the hood back over her head and gave Chance a leaping roundhouse kick that sent him tumbling.

She placed the end of her bo staff beneath Chance's chin, daring him to rise.

"You are a fool to be in our territory," the blue girl spat. "And right at nightfall, too. Do you have a death wish?"

"I'm sorry. I don't—"

Suddenly the girl's eyes grew wide with fear. Without explanation, she turned and ran, her quarrel with Chance forgotten.

"Shadowmen!" she screamed.

Chance turned to see what had so frightened his attacker. Ghostly shadows flew through the sky toward him. Their faces bore no distinguishable features save for the glowing crimson eyes housed beneath each of their furrowed brows. The sight of the Shadowmen conjured up thoughts of every boogeyman and monster Chance believed had lived under his bed as a boy. He shivered with fear.

"Run!" Chance screamed as he sheathed his billy clubs. "Outlaws, run!"

At Chance's words, the Outlaws, though still groggy from their thumping at the hands of the blue-skinned girl, bolted as a single unit toward the end of the canyon. They made it out only to realize they were at the edge of yet another cliff—one that had no bottom.

Chance turned, but the Shadowmen blocked the canyon mouth, cutting the Outlaws off from any hope of escape. Chance determined there were at least a dozen of them. He now saw they were humanoid and varied in size and shape in every way possible. But their ominous red eyes and viscous black skin chilled Chance to the bone.

One of the Shadowmen stepped forward and seized Psy-chick, effortlessly lifting her off the ground. Chance ran forward, but Shocker, finally showing some semblance of his old self, reached her attacker first.

"Get away from her, you parasites!" he yelled. "You bunch of nothings!"

A backhand from a neighboring Shadowman sent Shocker hurtling backward. He slammed into Space Cadet and both of them went tumbling over the edge of the cliff to the dark depths below.

Time seemed to slow as Chance watched his teammates go over.

"No!" he screamed, but he was too late.

Chance renewed his charge for Psy-chick. But like Shocker before him, his attempt was in vane. A Shadowman, this one feminine in form, lifted her arm and an energy bolt left her hand to strike Chance square in the chest. The Outlaw captain stumbled backward and gasped in horror as the feeling of earth beneath his feet disappeared.

Forgive me, Psy-chick, Chance thought as he tumbled over the cliff.

3

It seemed to Chance as though he'd been falling for all eternity; that his life back in Littleton with his family and his mentor, Captain Fearless, had all been just a dream, and this never-ending plummet into the abyss was the grim reality of existence.

However, where Chance's thoughts failed him, his training came to his rescue. Moving on instinct, his hand unsheathed the grappling gun holstered along his right thigh and fired its hook into the rock face speeding by.

The hook caught and pain seared through Chance's arms and shoulders as the line abruptly went taut. Chance transferred his momentum into his swing and somersaulted onto a small ledge along the cliff face, simultaneously thumbing the grappling gun's release and reel buttons and drawing both the hook and its line back inside the gun.

Chance looked up in shocked amazement to see a hulking

Shadowman looming over the blue-skinned girl who'd given him so much trouble back in the canyon.

Sucks to be you! Chance thought and turned to duck and run inside a cave leading into the cliff face. But a shrill scream from the girl halted him in his tracks.

"Flarn it!" Chance said as he whirled and leaped onto the Shadowman's back. The creature was unaffected by his attack, so he withdrew two pellet-sized concussion bombs from his utility belt and slammed them into the Shadowman's ears before dropping to the ground and scrambling backward on his elbows.

The bombs detonated and the Shadowman gave an inhuman wail of agony. He whirled on Chance, the girl forgotten, and closed the distance between them at an incredible rate of speed. The Shadowman seized Chance by his neck and hoisted him into the air. The touch of its ichor-covered hand felt like worms wriggling over his skin.

Chance watched in horror as the ichor lining the Shadowman's jaws formed into a worming proboscis that groped for his face. Just before it reached his nostrils, Chance thrust his right hand before his face. The proboscis met his gloved palm and pain like an icy fire engulfed his hand.

The Shadowman shrieked in frustration and thrust Chance against the cliff face, knocking the wind from his lungs. Chance heard something in the back of his utility belt break on impact. Suddenly bright, white light flashed from behind Chance, encircling him in a corona. The Shadowman gave a deafening shriek of pain and released Chance as he stumbled backward.

As the Shadowman writhed in agony, the ichor syrup covering his body drew back, retreating away from the light, revealing the person beneath—a grotesque figure with a large tusk jutting upward on either side of a snotty, wrinkled snout.

"Watch out," Chance said as the light strobe at his back faded, "You're going to—"

In his fit, the Shadowman ran off the ledge and plunged to the depths below. Chance was so shocked by this, it took him a moment to realize the blue girl had pulled him into the cave. She tugged him into a low crevice just large enough to slide in on one's belly.

When Chance regained enough of his senses, the blue girl gestured for him to be quiet. He did not have to wait long to find out why.

Even in their hiding place, Chance felt the displacement of air as Shadowmen landed on the ledge outside. They made no sound as they hovered in, the tips of their toes barely touching the cave floor.

The crimson eyes of several Shadowmen flashed in a way familiar to Chance. He'd seen it happen many times back at Burlington when students with the ability to see light at both ends of the electromagnetic spectrum invisible to human eyes activated their powers.

Not good, Chance thought nervously. It was only a matter of time before they were discovered.

Chance gasped in fear. The blue-skinned girl clamped her hand over his mouth and threw her cloak over his body. Chance watched breathless from beneath as the eyes of one of the Shadowmen peered directly at their hiding place . . . and then looked away.

Slowly, one by one, the Shadowmen exited the cavern, seemingly content that there was nothing to be found inside. They'd been gone for quite some time when, at last, the blue-skinned girl removed her hand and allowed Chance to breathe.

4

Psy-chick knew she was dreaming, but it didn't make seeing Chance, Shocker, and SC going over the cliff's edge all over again any easier. She watched, helpless in her dream, as the Shadowmen seized Private Justice, Iron Maiden, and Gothika and put them to sleep with a pale green flash from their bloodred eyes. Psy-chick screamed as the eyes of her own captor flashed green and darkness swallowed her.

Then the dream started over for what seemed like the hundredth time. The nightmarish memory played again and again until Psy-chick was certain she would go mad if she didn't wake up. But when at last she did awaken, terror overtook her, for she realized she wasn't going crazy—she *was already there*. She had to be. Only an insane mind could have imagined the scene that lay before her.

At first, Psy-chick had felt warm wind blowing against her face. The sensation had actually been pleasant until its scent reached her nose and she began to cough. The air was full of smoke and it stank of burning rubber.

She looked down to see she was flying hundreds of feet above a scorched landscape littered with plumes of fire billowing from pipes protruding from the ground. Machines that looked like gigantic horse-head pumps rose and fell, feeding the flames with each plunge.

The view was horrific and Psy-chick turned her head away from it to see her unconscious teammates flying alongside her in the arms of their Shadowmen captors. It was only then that Psy-chick registered she was also in the arms of a flying Shadowman. She looked up at him and gasped, but he paid her no notice. His bloody gaze was locked on the horizon.

Scared out of her mind, Psy-chick slowly turned her head to see where they were going. That's when she saw it—a gargantuan, spiraling tower so black it was even darker than the night sky surrounding it. It stood in the center of the flaming pyres, bolts of green lightning snaking from its surface to that of the four pylons standing like giant, up-turned nails at its quarters.

A moat of what looked like crude oil surrounded the fortress at its base. Psy-chick screamed as she saw two behemoth-sized monsters rise from the moat and roar at them. They were exactly like the one Chance had vanquished at the end of their first semester at Burlington. They snapped their fanged tentacles at Psy-chick before plunging back beneath the moat of ichor—the same ichor they and the Shadowmen wore as skin. The monster that Chance had bested had called itself Legion and claimed to be many. Psy-chick filled with despair at the realization that Legion had been telling the truth.

She heard her teammates utter their own cries of terror as they awakened to behold their present circumstances. On instinct, she tried to reach out to them with both head and heart, hoping to calm them down and soothe their fears. But there was only a hole in the place where her mind normally flexed, and that emptiness left her feeling more helpless than ever.

In moments, they were at the fortress. Its enormity overwhelmed Psy-chick's senses. She'd never seen anything so big in her entire life.

The Shadowmen's eyes flashed and a hangar-sized opening appeared in the tower's exterior. They flew inside and continued down a dark corridor to a room filled with black, table-shaped racks. The Shadowmen shoved the Outlaws down on top of them, taking little care. Ichor snaked out of the racks, forming into metal restraints that locked around the Outlaws' wrists, ankles, torsos, and foreheads.

Psy-chick screamed in terror as her captor moved toward her, his face forming into a searching proboscis.

"No! No!" she heard a human-sounding voice reprimand. "The master wants them left alone. We think she's the one!"

The Shadowman withdrew then squalled in agony before disintegrating into thin air.

A gigantic shadow filled Psy-chick's field of vision.

"Sleep," a thunderous voice commanded.

Overwhelmed with fear and confusion, Psy-chick obeyed.

5

Chance followed the blue-skinned girl deeper into the labyrinth of caves that had begun with their cramped hiding place. She held out a jar of bioluminescent beetles she'd gathered from the cave walls to light their way.

"I need to get back to my friends," Chance insisted. They'd been walking for what seemed like hours.

"If the Shadowmen have them," the girl said, "then forget it. They're gone. There's nothing you can do for them."

"I refuse to believe that," Chance said.

"Refuse until the Old Ones return from their graves. It changes nothing."

"I *will* find them," Chance said, hoping he sounded more confident than he felt.

"Is that your power?" the girl asked.

"Excuse me?" Chance asked as he massaged his right

hand. The place where the Shadowman had struck him still burned with a cold fire.

"That flash of light when the General attacked you. Is that your superpower?"

"Uh, General—?"

"It's what we Morlocks call those who have been Shadowmen so long that they can make others. Most can't do that. They are merely soldiers. But when they hunt, they always bring a General along in the lead. Anyway, the light?"

Chance hesitated, and then decided to answer truthfully.

"The UV flare isn't a superpower. It's just something I carry in my utility belt. I've only got one left.

"Normally, a person can't actually see ultraviolet light, but I had MOTHER add the white flash so I could be sure it was working if and when I set it off."

"Mother?"

"No, not mother, MOTHER—Mechanized Omnitasking Education Regulator. She's the quantum computer that basically runs Burlington Academy and outfits all its students."

"Is this Academy what you call the cave that you and your gang live in?"

"Sort of. But it's not a cave. It's a school. For superhumans. Its managing board members are the captains of The Brotherhood of Heroes—"

The blue girl whirled on Chance, raised her bo staff, and yelled at the top of her lungs.

What the . . . ? Chance thought. *She's attacking me!* He caught her bo staff just before she could bring it down on his head.

"Hey! What gives?" Chance asked.

"How dare you mention the name of the jailers," the girl said, "the accursed ones who abandoned our parents to this unholy place!"

"Wait a minute. Your parents? You, the hunchback, and the bat-thing? You're the offspring of the supervillains sentenced to the Shadow Zone, aren't you?"

"Your kind called them supervillains, but their only crime was not bowing down before the self-proclaimed authority of the Brotherhood!"

The blue girl crossed her arms.

"And now, thanks to your precious *Heroes*, they've been taken by the hundreds and assimilated into the ranks of the Shadowmen. That warthog-man beneath the ichor, once upon a time he was one of us!"

"And I killed him," Chance whispered, his eyes wide beneath his mask.

"Trust me," the girl said, "if he died in that fall, which I doubt—we couldn't be that lucky—you did him a favor."

Dear heaven, Chance thought. *If all this is true . . .*

"This all has to be a terrible mistake. There's no way the Brotherhood would exile people here if they knew about the Shadowmen."

"Don't be so sure! But ignorance is no excuse for what occurs here! I've seen countless mothers and fathers ripped from the arms of their children. And I've seen those same children come of age only to share their parents' fate." Tears swelled within the blue girl's eyes. "Even my own brother!"

The blue girl dropped her staff and squatted to the

ground, placing her sobbing face in her knees as she hugged herself.

Slowly, cautiously, Chance approached and patted her cloaked back.

"I . . ." Chance began, thinking of the father taken from him by suicide. "I know what it's like to lose a family member."

The thought of his departed father opened a door within Chance, one he'd slammed shut a long time ago. Visions of Shocker and SC going over the cliff began to play within his mind. Tears of grief began to run from his eyes and it wasn't long before his body shook with sobs.

It's all my fault, Chance thought. *They were my best friends and now they're gone! If only I'd been a better captain. I could've saved you!*

"What's the matter, Chance?"

Chance looked up in disbelief to see Space Cadet and Shocker standing over him, the hunchback and the bat-person at their backs.

"Please, Chance," Shocker sobbed as he removed his sunglasses and wiped his electricity-barren eyes. "If you don't stop crying, I can't either."

6

Chance leaped from the ground and wrapped Space Cadet and Shocker in his arms.

"You're alive!" he said as he hugged them to him. "It's a miracle!"

"They saved us, Chance," SC said as he gestured toward the hunchback and the bat-boy.

"And then led us here," Shocker added.

"The miracle is that I managed to stay aloft when I snatched your chubby friend out of the air," the bat-boy said. His accent held a hint of British cockney. "That one could do to miss a meal or two, so he could."

Chance was grinning ear to ear when he felt Shocker plant a slobbery kiss on his cheek.

"Hey!" Chance said as he drew back. "I'm glad you're alive, Shocker, but take it easy!"

"I'm sorry, Chance," Shocker said, his teary-eyed grin

equaling Chance's own. "I couldn't help it." Shocker's voice, full of emotion, caught in his throat. "You were just so happy to see us!"

"Shocker," Chance said, tilting his head in question, "Don't take this the wrong way, man, but what's gotten into you?"

"He's been like this since he showed up with Brutus," Space Cadet said.

"Brutus catch crybaby!" Brutus announced proudly.

"Niagara Falls one minute," SC continued, "flowers and sunshine the next."

"I know, I know," Shocker said, wiping the last of the tears from his eyes. "I'm sorry. I can't help it. All these thoughts and emotions—it's overwhelming. I don't see how Psy-chick does it."

"Does what, Shocker?" Chance asked, suspicion beginning to form.

"Chance," Shocker began, "I think somehow, when we teleported here—I don't know if it was crossing the dimensional barrier or what—but I think things got mixed up."

"Go on," Chance said.

"Ever since we arrived in the Shadow Zone," Shocker said, "I've been able to hear everyone's thoughts. Everyone's but yours, that is. I've caught quite a few mental shouts from you. Heck, all our minds have been screaming with fear and confusion from the moment we integrated here. But for the most part, your noggin' is sealed up pretty tight.

"Anyways, what I'm trying to say is, I know right now SC

is thinking about how he wishes he was back on Mars eating one of his mother's Barsoomberry pies."

Space Cadet nodded. "It's true."

"And I can feel the relief radiating from all of us that we're poking around down here in the caves instead of being covered in black Shadowman goop."

"Amen to that," the bat-boy said.

"What I'm saying is, when we teleported, I lost my powers, but gained Psy-chick's psionic abilities."

Chance tapped his chin with his finger, considering. "Thoughts, SC? Do you have any idea how this could've happened?"

"No," Space Cadet grimaced in thought. "But I should." SC scratched the back of his white plastic helmet. "The thing is, I know, normally, I'd have all kinds of hypotheses on what's going on. I mean, other than you, Chance, I'm the resident whiz kid, right?"

Space Cadet gesticulated in frustration as he spoke. "But when I try to think about it, things just get all jumbled up in my head. It's like trying to remember something you know is filed somewhere in your brain, but it just won't come!

"And that's not the only thing. I always carry spare parts in my costume, in case I need to assemble some gadget on the fly, which we all know happens often.

"Normally I can *hear* the pieces chatting or humming as I carry them. But since we arrived in the Shadow Zone, it's just like my communicator watch: crickets and tumbleweeds. Not a word spoken from them! Whatever it is that's affected Shocker has taken away my powers of technomancy."

"Well, Shocker seems to have traded powers," Chance said. "Or at least lost his own and gained Psy-chick's. Have you manifested anyone else's power?" Chance asked.

"Not yet," SC said. "However, it was flarn lucky Shocker and I survived that fall." SC snapped his gloved fingers and his face lit up. "That's it! I bet I've got your power of super good luck."

That would be a good trick, Chance thought, *considering I made that power up to fool everyone.*

"That's . . ." Chance began, carefully choosing his words, "one possibility. I guess we'll just have to wait to see for sure."

"What about you, Chance?" Shocker asked. "Stretching like PJ? Conjuring like Gothika?"

Chance shrugged. "Not as of yet."

"What about the others?" Shocker asked. "Maybe they managed to escape like us. Did you see any sign of them on your way here?"

Chance frowned and shook his head.

"We've got to go after them," SC said.

"That's a fact, SC," Chance agreed. "I don't know how we're going to find them, but we've got to try."

"Enough talk," the blue girl said. "Your friends are gone! Be glad the masked one aided me against the General or I'd get rid of the rest of you, myself. Now, let's move."

The Outlaws looked at one another and shrugged, having little choice but to obey their present . . . benefactors? Jailers? Chance wasn't sure yet.

7

"Old Ones keep us!" the blue-skinned girl said. "Did your friend have to take the deepest tunnel he could find to relieve himself?"

Chance shrugged. "Can I help it if he's discovered modesty within the last few hours?"

"You're right," Shocker said as he emerged from an adjoining cave, "it was very insensitive of me to take so long. My sincerest apologies."

Chance and Space Cadet grinned. They knew the drill. That was Shocker's setup. Next would come one of his trademark snappy comebacks to knock it home. However, their grins disappeared when Shocker simply walked on ahead of them without a word.

"I guess having Psy-chick's powers has matured him." Chance said. He and SC peered at each other in silence.

"We've got to fix this," SC said.

"Yeah. And fast!"

The six of them continued on with the blue girl in the lead. Chance noticed clouds of steam venting from holes in the walls at various points. *Geothermal venting,* Chance thought. *That's how it stays so warm down here.*

Without looking back at them, the blue girl halted and raised her hand, gesturing for them to stop.

"It's me," the blue girl said, "Viz."

"Who's she talking to?" Space Cadet asked.

"All of them," Shocker said.

"All of—"

Cloaked figures appeared out of the shadows all around them. Most of them were dwarfish in size, but that's where their physical similarities ended. A different nose, snout, beak, or muzzle poked out from beneath every hood.

More supervillain offspring, Chance thought.

He was surprised to see a scattering of ancient Viking battle axes, Roman short swords, and medieval shields clutched in their hands, tentacles, and claws. Those who were not armed glowed with various forms of colored energy.

Oh crap! Chance thought as he took a fighting stance. We're outnumbered ten to one! "Outlaws," Chance called, "to me!"

The blue-skinned girl sighed and rolled her eyes.

"Specs?" one of the taller cloaked figures said.

He was answered by one of the smallest. "On it!" Specs' voice was high-pitched and unmistakably young. He looked Viz up and down through a pair of eyeglasses so thick they made his pupils look like manhole covers.

"I've scanned her DNA, Mace," Specs said. He reached beneath his hood and adjusted his bifocals. "If she's a shape-shifter, it's the finest transformation I've ever seen. Much too sophisticated for a Shadowman. Even a General."

The one called Mace pulled back his hood to reveal the face of an athletic-looking human male in his teens. He stepped up to the blue-skinned girl whose name had been revealed to be Viz. Without warning, he struck out at her with his right hand. Only it wasn't a hand at the end of his arm, but a literal spike-tipped mace.

Viz expertly dodged the blow and then caught another from Mace's left with her bo staff before he halted his attack.

"It's her," Mace said as the weapons at his wrists transformed into hands. "Who's this you've brought with you? More Uruks in our territory? Little Coffin Hunters maybe? We Morlocks will grind them up and send them back in a box."

Shocker gulped and then whispered to Chance and SC. "He means it."

"They're not Uruks," Viz said, "Death Eaters, Low Men, or any of the other hundreds of gangs we know. They call themselves 'Outlaws,' like our parents before us. And like our parents, they claim to have come from Earth."

At the mention of Earth, reverent whispers spread through the crowd.

"*They're with the Brotherhood,*" Viz continued, and the whispers were quickly replaced by shouts of outrage.

"Blast them!"

"Pound them!"

"Wipe their minds!"

The last went up as a chant among the crowd until Viz hurled her bo staff like a spear to strike the jar of beetles held aloft by one of the taller youths in attendance. The jar shattered with a loud crash, spilling light-filled beetles to the cavern floor. The sound silenced the mob. Viz's bo staff rebounded twice off the cave walls before bouncing back to rest in her hand.

"You know I have no love for the Brotherhood," Viz said, projecting her voice. "Be that as it may, this one saved my life." Viz pointed her staff at Chance. "From a General, no less."

The crowd gasped at Chance.

"Can any among us claim such a feat?" Viz waited. No reply came. "He and his companions deserve a chance to be heard. It's the least we can do." Viz turned and looked at Chance, her face sharpening as though she were bringing him into focus. "It's more than the Brotherhood ever granted our parents."

"Take them to Caesar," Mace said.

"Caesar will know what to do," Specs agreed. Their comments were echoed by the crowd, and before long, Viz was once again leading Chance and his friends through the caverns. Only now it was with a hostile mob at their backs and a meeting with a stranger who held their lives in the balance ahead of them.

8

Psy-chick awoke, images of giant shadows and thunderous voices (*Sleep*) playing in her mind. Psy-chick shook her head, deciding not to dwell upon such any further. She had more pressing things to worry about. Namely, finding Iron Maiden, Gothika, and Private Justice.

The thoughts of her friends brought the memory of Chance, Shocker, and Space Cadet going over the cliff edge surging to the forefront of her mind.

The three of them are dead, she thought. *SC, Shocker . . . Chance . . . all dead.*

Psy-chick caught herself before the sobs could start.

And you and the others may join them if you don't get control of yourself and figure out how to get out of here!

Psy-chick wiped her eyes. She raised up on her elbows and saw she was lying on top of a luxurious bed in a room worthy of a queen. Everywhere she looked, golden finery met her eyes. The room's furniture was made of jewel-encrusted ivory wreathed with still more gold, and ornate purple drapes hung about the room.

Psy-chick leaped from the bed, ran to the room's edge, and threw back a pair of the drapes. The windows she'd hoped to see there were absent. She found only life-sized reliefs carved into the gilded walls.

Psy-chick rushed around the room, pulling back the other drapes. But no windows were to be found. The carvings continued the entire length of the circular room save for a bejeweled door directly opposite the bed.

Psy-chick tried the door's knob. She was surprised when it turned without protest. She pulled the door slightly open, taking care to make as little noise as possible. She peered into the adjoining room. An enormous banquet table overflowing with hot, steaming food met her eyes and her stomach rumbled so loud she jerked back, certain the sound would bring every Shadowman within twelve miles running.

She held her breath and waited, her body a coiled spring. But no one came. After some time, she gained enough confidence to step into the room. It was larger than the other, but somehow cozier. It was decorated with equal majesty, but along with the food-covered table, it housed a large, comfortable-looking chair that sat beside a grand hearth. Both items would have been right at home within some rich, European nobleman's study.

Psy-chick startled when a small fire sprang to life within

the hearth. The fire threw Psy-chick's shadow on the wall before her. It flickered and jumped, gigantic one moment, dwarfish the next.

Psy-chick walked over to the banquet table, her stomach practically doing leaps in anticipation of the feast that lay before her. She picked up a single glossy red apple, studied it, and then, before she could think about it any further, her mouth moved of its own accord and bit down.

The taste was so delicious that it bordered on ecstasy. She quickly consumed the piece of fruit and then helped herself to bites of roasted pheasant, succulent greens, various cheeses, and chocolates of every description, washing it all down with a goblet of some sweet, buttery liquid. It was undoubtedly the finest meal she had ever eaten.

When at last she finished, Psy-chick waddled to the fireside chair and sank down into it, full and content. It was then that she spied the most beautiful gown ever to meet her eyes.

Had the dress been there when she entered the room? Psy-chick couldn't recall. She didn't think so. But then she only had eyes for the food when she had come in.

It hung on an obsidian mannequin exactly her size and shape that stood beside a full-length, oval mirror in the room's center. The gown was black, but covered with sparkling diamonds. It was open at the shoulders and ravens' feathers were sown onto it for trim.

A gown fit for a princess, Psy-chick thought. *A princess of night.*

Why not put it on? Psy-chick was startled to hear her own mind form the question. She argued with herself. I don't dare. But it's so beautiful. What would it hurt? It might even help. Who's to say all the ladies here don't wear these? It might serve as a disguise.

Not needing to convince herself further, Psy-chick removed the dress from the mannequin. The mannequin seemed to shed the gown of its own accord for her, and Psy-chick would have sworn she felt someone redirect her hand to free the dress when it snagged briefly during removal.

Though she thought herself alone, Psy-chick stepped behind an ornate folding partition conveniently located in the room's corner to change.

Had it been here all along, too?

Psy-chick wasn't sure. She decided it wasn't worth considering.

The dress slipped on easily and felt like the finest of silks against her body. Psy-chick came out from behind the partition and peered at herself in the mirror. She gasped as the dress flowed like water down her arms to form draping sleeves and up the back of her neck to form a high feathered collar. Jewels blossomed along the cloth to form a necklace of sparkling diamonds at her throat. The gown's magic continued along her face, covering her mouth in ebony lipstick and lengthening her eyelashes with wisps of inky night.

Gothika would absolutely love this! Psy-chick thought. Then another thought came to her mind—one cold and unfamiliar: Sour grapes to Gothika, you look amazing, my dear!

Psy-chick smiled as she admired herself in the glass, knowing it was true. Then she screamed, her mood changing to stark terror as, gazing into the mirror, she saw the reflection of her fire-spawned shadow leave its place on the wall and press toward her.

9

"Move!"

Chance felt someone shove him in the back. He stumbled forward into an enormous cavern full of light so bright he had to shield his eyes. He lowered his hand and saw that they'd reached the Morlocks' home. It was a small village of round domiciles literally carved out of the cavern's rock wall.

Definitely the work of superhuman hands, Chance thought.

The light that had blinded him upon entry came predominantly from large rock pillars that lined the village pathways like streetlamps.

Electric light, here? Chance thought.

His eyes focused. He saw hordes of bioluminescent beetles crawling over one another inside the honeycombed pillars.

Makes sense.

"Mo—!"

Chance whirled and caught Mace's hand before it could give him another shove.

"Do that again and you'll have to change your name from Mace to Stumpy!"

Mace scowled at him but said nothing. Chance turned his back to him, confident no more shoves would come.

They made their way down the cavern slope and entered the village. The Morlocks came out in droves to watch their passing. They were every size and shape imaginable, but Chance could tell by their appearance that the eldest of them was fourteen, at most.

The younger ones rushed out to scrutinize them. They tugged at Chance's utility belt, plucked at SC's spandex, and jerked on Shocker's coat. The Outlaws knew better than to resist these minor annoyances.

Chance gazed at the back of Viz's head as she greeted her fellow Morlocks.

If what she says is true, Chance thought, *the ones our age are on borrowed time, just waiting to be picked off in the next Shadowman recruitment drive!*

Chance pondered this. Why do they go after the adults and teenagers but leave the children alone? It must be because of something that happens to them during adolescence.

"That's when their powers come to full fruition," Shocker said as he righted his bandanna from where a particularly curious young Morlock had pulled it down over his nose. Chance snapped his head in his friend's direction.

"Sorry, Chance," Shocker continued, "but you where

thinking pretty loudly right then. But it's the truth. Take her for instance—" Shocker nodded to a wolf-girl peeking out at them bashfully from behind a makeshift door. "She transformed for the first time just this morning. Now she's terrified that the Shadowmen are going to come for her. And she's just the tip of the iceberg. Fear and worry hangs over this place so thick you could cut it with a knife!"

"It's not right," Chance said. "No one should have to live their lives in constant fear."

Viz abruptly turned to face them.

She pointed at Chance. "You come with me. Your friends stay here with Mace."

Chance raised his eyebrow in question to Shocker.

Shocker nodded. "Her thoughts don't seem to indicate she means you any immediate harm."

"All right," Chance said. "Let's go."

"Come on, Brutus," Viz said. He nodded enthusiastically and fell in step with the two of them as they approached a large orb-shaped building in the town's center. *Morlock City Hall,* Chance decided. Its doorway was blocked by a giant boulder.

"Brutus, if you please," Viz said, but Brutus was already at the stone, the muscles of his tremendous arms rising and falling like ocean waves as he rolled it away from the building's entrance.

Once they were inside the building, Brutus tugged the rock back into place. The building's interior was constituted by a single round room already alight with beetle-shine.

Chance scanned the room, but saw no one other than Viz and Brutus.

Maybe Caesar's invisible, Chance thought, *or microscopic.* He'd seen superhumans with similar powers back at Burlington.

"Brutus," Viz said, "we need to talk to Caesar."

"Okay, Viz." Brutus walked to the center of the room and turned his back to them. Then he raised his arms above his head and removed the cloak blanketing his body.

Chance was flabbergasted to see that the hump at Brutus's back was not a hump at all, but a head—an extremely large, bald head. Two misshapen, vestigial arms sprouted from Brutus's back just beneath it. They stirred and Brutus's second head opened its massive, jaundiced eyes and gave a large exhale of air. Its breath smelled of gingersnaps, and Chance found it oddly pleasant.

"Vision," Caeser said, his voice a rough whisper, "why have you disobeyed the Code and brought a stranger into our most secret place?"

Viz bowed slightly. "Caesar, I beg your forgiveness. This one is no threat to us. He claims to be from Earth and I believe him.

"He saved me from a General, though he had the opportunity to flee. To abandon him after that would have made me no better than the Uruks, and I am a Morlock who abides by the Code.

Caesar squinted, considering. "Very well. What is his name?"

"He is—"

"I am Chance Fortune of the Outlaws. Like you, my friends and I are trapped in the Shadow Zone. We have had our loved ones taken from us by the Shadowmen."

"Then, like us," Caesar said, "your fate is to despair. For the Shadow Prince and his minions rule this land, and what they take, they do not return."

"Shadow Prince?" Chance asked.

Caesar raised one of his small, twisted arms. Chance watched breathless as the beetle-light gathered from the corners of the room into a single, swirling mass before Caesar's outstretched palm. The light formed into a shimmering hologram of a majestic white city surrounded by lush green forest.

"Once this dimension was home to the Old Ones—an ancient race who knew only peace and prosperity. It is from their recovered writings that we learned of the Code."

The hologram changed to showcase beings of pure light tending strange animals and cultivating dense woodlands. "They achieved untold technological wonders while maintaining harmony with the natural world."

Suddenly, storm clouds formed within the hologram, eclipsing all other images from view. "Then the Shadow Prince came and obliterated their light and love from existence."

A bolt of cold pain seared through Chance's right hand. He grabbed his wrist and squeezed as he gritted his teeth.

"He infected this world with his evil," Caesar continued. "He corrupted its life and its lands."

The image changed to display an ominous black shadow covering the sun. "He even wages war against the sun, working to blot out its life-giving warmth."

Chance's hand throbbed with ache. He bit down on his lip so hard he drew blood.

"The days grow shorter with each one that passes," Caesar continued. "When at last they are no more, the Shadowmen will roam the land unchecked and their prince will hold sway over all."

The hologram changed to show a towering geyser of ichor with a single large red eye at its apex. As Chance looked upon it, the pain in his hand exploded up his arm with such force that he yelled and dropped to his knees.

The hologram dissipated. "Show me your hand," Caesar commanded. When Chance did not comply, Viz took hold of it and yanked it out for Caesar to examine.

"You have been infected," Caesar said, his yellow eyes wide.

"By your reaction," Chance said as he yanked his wrist from Viz's hand and got to his feet, his pain now abating, "I'm guessing this is something a few antibiotics won't be able to cure."

Viz nodded, a look of pity on her face.

"So how do I get rid of it?" Chance asked. "What's the cure?"

"There's only one known cure for shadowbite," Caesar said. "*Death.*"

10

Psy-chick whirled to face the living shadow, her fear eclipsing her scream. The Shadow-thing pressed toward her, snaking away from the wall as red light gathered to form a dreadful cyclopean eye at its forefront. Psy-chick backed away. The backs of her knees hit the lounge chair and she collapsed into it, trembling as the massive shadow-thing came to loom over her. It positioned its eye within inches of her face.

"Do I frighten you?" the shadow-thing asked. Its mouthless voice was the low rumble of distant thunder.

Psy-chick gasped and nodded her head so enthusiastically the raven's feathers serving as her gown's collar could have taken flight.

The shadow-thing chuckled. The deep bass tone of its laughter rattled Psy-chick's teeth. "Then perhaps this form will be more to your liking."

Psy-chick heard another sound, one similar to that of water being poured into a bucket, and the shadow-thing changed before her eyes. Its bulk swirled and diminished until it was not a monster of ichor before her, but Chance himself. He was dressed in a T-shirt and jeans the color of shadow rather than his battle dress uniform.

"Chance?" Psy-chick asked.

The figure before her opened his eyes, and the brief hope Psy-chick had allowed herself vanished. The Chance-thing's eyes glowed bloodred like those of the Shadowmen. It was not Chance before her, but the monster merely dressed in a Chance-shaped husk.

"Do you approve?" the shadow-thing asked, a sardonic grin across its new face. It now spoke with a dark parody of Chance's voice.

"N-n-no!" Psy-chick said, finding her voice at last. "Change back. Or into something else."

The shadow-thing looked down at its new body and ran its hands admiringly over its chest and down the sides of its abdomen. "No. This one fits surprisingly well. I believe I'll keep it for a while."

"You may look like Chance," Psy-chick said, "but you're not him. Who are you?"

The shadow-thing's grin widened as the brow above his crimson eyes furrowed. "I've had many names over the centuries. My subjects in this realm call me the Shadow Prince.

"But you may call me Mordred. I came across the name while researching Earth's culture and, like your friend's appearance, I think it suits my person most aptly."

"Your soldiers killed them." There was no strength in Psy-chick's voice. Only despair.

"Ah, yes, your dear captain and his two closest lieutenants. A regrettable accident, I assure you. Such gross negligence is inexcusable in my Shadowmen. Rest assured I have dealt with the guilty parties. They will never have the opportunity to run afoul again."

Mordred clasped his hands behind his back and leaned over Psy-chick. She scrambled backward, trying unsuccessfully to dig herself into the chair.

"How are you doing that?" Mordred asked, genuinely curious.

"Doing what?" Psy-chick asked, her voice quivering.

"Hiding your powers from me. I've looked over every atom in your entire body and found no trace of your psionic abilities."

"I've . . ." Psy-chick fumbled for words. "I've lost my powers."

Mordred straightened. "Tsk-tsk. You know what happens to liars don't you?"

Psy-chick shook her head.

"They go to the Shadow Zone." A sadistic grin crept over Mordred's face. "Oh, wait a minute. You're already here!"

Mordred broke into laughter. Psy-chick gulped.

Abruptly, Mordred stopped laughing and placed his hands on the chair's arms.

"Don't play games with me, Psy-chick. I know everything there is to know about you. Before you and that *boy* destroyed him, my minion downloaded files on every student, teacher, and administrator at Burlington Academy. Your power-potential is off the charts and you were the only one *not* to be assimilated by Legion."

He may be right, Psy-chick thought. *Chance and I were the only ones that monster failed to possess at school last semester.*

"There has only been one other like you in this century," Mordred continued, "but despite my best efforts, I've been unable to locate the boy called Murry. So, therefore, it must be you. Make no mistake, you are the key!"

"Key?" Psy-chick really didn't want to know, but she couldn't keep herself from asking.

Mordred stood and raised his hand. "Behold." The wall opposite the bedroom changed into wriggling black ooze that opened to reveal a stormhead-filled sky above the jacking pumps and billowing flames.

The floor beneath their feet raised and extended beyond the opening so that they were outside, miles above the terrain. Psy-chick wrapped her arms around the chair, holding on to it for dear life as she choked on the black smoke from the pyres.

"Morning comes," Mordred said. As if cued by his words, tiny rays from a half-eclipsed sun began to slice through the cloud-filled sky. Psy-chick looked back to Mordred. He stared at the approaching light, disgust in his eyes. Psy-chick thought she saw something else there, too—*fear.*

"So long as the sun shines within the sky to any measure," Mordred continued, "I am a prisoner in this infernal dimension."

Suddenly, the floor retracted, reeling them back inside the

fortress. The wall closed up of its own accord, eclipsing Psy-chick's view of the approaching dawn.

"My technomancer will rectify that problem soon enough," Mordred said, turning his gaze back on Psy-chick. "Even now his dark sciences draw this world's moons farther and farther across the sun's face. When the eclipse is complete, the barrier between this reality and all others will be at its weakest. I shall be able to escape from this dimension at long last!"

"Good," Psy-chick said. "You'll get what you want. I guess there's no reason for you to hold my friends and me here then."

Mordred smiled. "I'm afraid it's not that simple. Blotting out the sun is only half the solution to my problem.

"You see, things drop into the Shadow Zone all the time. Take you and your friends, for instance. It wasn't hard at all to subvert your teleport here. But the *getting out* . . . now, that's another story!"

"What's that got to do with me?"

Mordred sighed. He turned and walked toward a wall. At his approach, a window formed in its surface to reveal the stygian landscape below.

"We had to strip this world of half its resources in order to create a hole large enough to send Legion to your reality, and that only amounted to a pinprick in the dimensional barrier.

"It would take a billion times that amount of energy to crack the barrier wide enough to allow passage for a being of such metaphysical girth as myself, and that's power even I don't have." Mordred turned and narrowed his gaze on Psy-chick. "Until now, that is.

"In order to escape, I need a *key* to open a dimensional doorway for me—someone with unlimited psionic potential. In short, *I need you.*" The low rumble of thunder returned to Mordred's voice in full force as he spoke his last words. The sound vibrated through Psy-chick's body, driving out all semblance of hope it found there.

"Where are my friends?" Psy-chick asked, her voice trembling once again. "Where are Gothika, Justice, and Iron Maiden?"

Mordred grinned. "First, I should tell you it will be useless for you to go poking around in my mind for their location. I have had that knowledge buried so deep in my subconscious that even you will not be able to find it.

"But let me assure you, your friends are safe—for now."

Mordred's gaze narrowed.

"Cooperate, and they just might stay that way."

11

Chance shook his head as he massaged his hand. He looked about the orb-shaped room and then to Viz and Caesar in turn as if searching for an answer to his predicament.

"That can't be true," Chance said. "I don't know this Shadow Prince you speak of, but his power can't be absolute. There must be some way my friends and I can be saved. Surely, someone has—"

"Oh," Caesar said, his yellow eyes rolling toward Viz, "there have been those who tried. But the only thing they succeed in doing is adding their strength to that of the Shadowmen—giving that foul host yet another superpower to be shared by its ranks."

"That's why they can do all those things," Chance said. "Superspeed, flight, eye-beams. It's like the opposite of a negator. The Shadowmen don't cancel out powers, they absorb them and then share them with one another."

Viz nodded. "The Shadow Zone's sparse sunlight is the only thing that has allowed a few of us to evade capture."

"You're saying the Shadowmen can't endure sunlight?"

"Yes," Viz said. "It's toxic to them. But if they ever figure out how to withstand it—"

"They will be truly unstoppable," Caesar finished for her, "and shadow will reign over all."

"You could take the fight to them before that happens," Chance said. "Unite with the other gangs against your common enemy. If there are as many factions as you say roaming free within these caves, you could create a force that would give even the Shadowmen pause."

Caesar looked to Viz. She turned away, unable to bear his gaze. "Another once thought as you did," Caesar said. "The Shadow Prince rewarded his ambition with a special brand of cruelty. At any rate, to send children, even superpowered children, against an army of Shadowmen is madness."

"If the situation is as hopeless as you say," Chance said, "better to meet destiny on your feet than to cower in a cave." Chance shrugged. "Who knows? You might even win."

Caesar's gaze narrowed. "Only those with nothing to lose can afford to be so bold."

Chance looked down at his wounded hand. He could feel the coldness spreading even now, snaking its way beyond his wrist. The ultimate outcome of his injury was a thought his mind refused to consider. And that was just as well. Chance's friends needed him. His path was clear. Nothing else mattered.

"If I'm truly as good as dead," Chance said, "why not permit my friends and me to leave. We will look for our teammates on our own. And if you can spare provisions for our journey, you would have all the thanks that are ours to give."

"You saved Vision," Caesar said, "therefore, before I answer, I would like to put to you another option: rather than risking your lives on a fool's errand, you and your friends could stay with us."

"What about the infection?" Chance asked.

"We have healers in the village, those who could keep the shadow-poison at bay. At least for a time.

"At your age, you'd run the same risk of being taken by the Shadowmen that we all do. But if you evade capture, you might have several good years left before the shadow-bite consumes you. Why risk them to save those who have already fallen into shadow?"

"Because they are my friends," Chance said without hesitation, "and would do the same for me. Because, regardless, it is the right thing to do."

"I see," Caesar said. "Either you honor the Code in this, or you are the biggest fool I have ever met.

"I will grant you your request, though it will be a waste to do so. You will not last a day in the Shadow Zone on your own. The way to Shadow Tower is full of danger with or without the Shadowmen."

"Be that as it may," Chance said, "I must try."

Caesar nodded. "Then may the Old One have mercy upon you, Chance Fortune, for the Shadow Prince will not."

The three of them exited Morlock City Hall. As Chance and Viz approached the others, a recloaked Brutus rolled the stone door back into place.

"He called you Vision," Chance said as they walked side by side.

"Yeah," Viz said, tapping the ground with her bo staff every other step. "Everyone calls me Viz for short, but that's my power. I can see things just before they happen. It's what allows me to fight so well—I know what moves my opponents will make before they do."

"Kind of like spidey-sense."

"Pardon?"

"Never mind. Is the immediate future all that's open to you? Can you ever look further ahead?"

"Sometimes."

"What do you see happening to my friends and me?"

Viz's face darkened at the question. Chance decided to change the subject. "How far to the Shadow Prince's lair, his Shadow Tower?"

"Months taking the caves, especially going around the other gangs' territories."

"And by taking the surface?"

"Like Caesar said, the wastelands are a dangerous place. I wouldn't recommend traveling aboveground."

Chance frowned, impatient.

Viz sighed. "Taking the surface at night is suicide. That's when the Shadowmen hunt. But if you only traveled above while the sun shines and then below for a time after it sets, you could make it within a week, provided you managed to stay alive." Viz looked down at Chance's hand. "But it's likely the shadow-bite will consume you long before then."

Chance halted and grabbed Viz at the elbow. "Viz, promise me you won't tell my friends about the shadow-bite. Shocker, the one with the bandanna, can hear thoughts, so I need you to not think about it. Can you do that for me?"

Viz stared at Chance, then nodded. She turned and called to Mace. "Caesar has allowed them to go, Mace. They no longer need guarding."

Mace looked at Shocker and SC, grunted, and then stomped off.

Viz placed her hand on Chance's where he held her elbow. "I will see to your supplies."

"Thank you," Chance said. He felt like a person being served his final meal before being sent to the electric chair. Viz left him to gather their provisions. He turned and tried to put on a confident face for his friends.

"So what's up, Chance?" SC asked. "Are they going to help us find Maiden and the others?"

"No," Chance said. "But we're going to look for them anyway."

"Well, of course we are," Shocker said.

"Guys," Chance said, "I'm not going to lie to you. This is serious—"

"You're not about to launch into some speech about untold danger and possible death, are you, Hicksville?" Shocker asked. "If so, save your breath. We've got lost Outlaws out there and that's all that matters."

Chance shrugged. "SC?"

Space Cadet looked at his friends and then held out his hand, palm down. "Where angels fear to tread."

Chance and Shocker placed their hands on top of his. "Where angels fear to tread!"

12

"What the hurl was I thinking?" Shocker asked as he dropped his pack and collapsed onto the cavern floor. "Angels fear to tread my blurn! It sure was a lot easier going down than coming up!"

"Oh, quit whining, you big baby," Chance said as he turned from the cave exit. "It was only about fifteen miles to get here. Look at SC. He's not even winded."

"Yeah, Shocker," SC said. "That was a walk in the park compared to some of the training we've had at Burlington."

"Come on, man. Get up," Chance said, nudging Shocker's pack with his boot. "We're at the surface and we're burning daylight. And sunshine is a precious thing here in the Shadow Zone."

Shocker sighed and then slowly got to his feet. He hoisted

his pack onto his shoulder and fell in step behind SC and Chance. They exited the cave. The terrain was full of the rocky crags that hung beneath a dark gray sky.

"The Morlocks need to reset their clocks," Chance said as he peered up at the endless gray. "We should've arrived at high noon. But judging by the sky it's got to be near sundown."

"We told you correctly," Viz said. The Outlaws whirled in the direction of her voice, shocked to see her among them. It was as though she had just materialized out of a cluster of nearby boulders. "It is noon. This is as bright as it gets since the Shadow Prince came to power."

"What are you doing here?" Chance asked.

"You forgot your chameleon-cloaks." Viz threw open her cloak and pitched the clothing she'd been carrying underneath it at the Outlaw's feet. They picked them up, dusted them off, and inspected them.

"These were specially woven by our fabricmancer," Viz continued. "They won't shield you out in the open, but hide yourself within the terrain, and you'll be as good as invisible. Even from the Shadowmen."

Chance nodded, thinking about how Viz's cloak had hidden them from the Shadowmen in their first encounter, how the cloaked Morlocks had been able to sneak up on them in the caves, and how Viz had seemingly walked through sheer rock just now.

"The cloaks also help guard against the Shadow Zone's harsh elements," Viz said as she watched the Outlaws put theirs on. "And that's something you're definitely going to need."

"Thanks," Shocker said, a knowing look in his eye, "but you didn't travel all this way just to give us a special parting-gift, did you?"

Viz stood in silence for a moment, a stern look on her face. "No. The maps we gave you, while the best we have, are ancient. You'll need a guide. Someone who's been close to Shadow Tower. And that just happens to be me."

"What were you doing near Shadow Tower?" SC asked.

"It none of your concern," Viz snapped. "If you are going to waste my time with questions, find Shadow Tower yourselves!" She strode several yards away to be alone.

"Touch-ee!" SC said, rolling his eyes.

After a moment, Shocker walked over to Viz and placed his hand on her shoulder.

"Empathy's not my bag, Viz," he said. "I've never been much good at caring about anyone but myself. But right now my marbles are all scrambled and I can't help but feel your pain—and know the reason for it.

"So trust me when I say if anyone can get our friends *and* your brother out of this mess, it's that guy over there."

Shocker pointed his thumb in Chance's direction. "I've seen him single-handedly take down demigods and world-conquering aliens. This Shadow Prince will be just another notch in Chance's belt when it's all said and done. You'll see."

"Do you really believe that?" Viz asked.

Shocker tilted his head and grinned. "Maybe. He vanquished a General, didn't he? You said it yourself: no one's ever done that before, right?"

Viz nodded reluctantly.

"All I really know," Shocker continued, "is that he's naïve enough to think we can save our friends. Considering how many times I've seen Chance beat the odds, who am I to argue?"

Viz stood in silence considering, then abruptly called over her shoulder. "We head south." Without another word, she was off, her bo staff leading the way as a walking stick.

"What did you say to get her to be our guide again?" SC asked as he and Chance joined Shocker.

Shocker grinned. "Sorry, SC. You've got to scrub the calluses from her feet every night."

"What?"

"Sorry, pud. It was the only way."

"Aaah, man!"

SC slumped and stuck out his bottom lip as he waddled away. Chance and Shocker looked at each other, failing in their attempts to hold back their laughter.

Chance and the others looked at the scene before them with horror and disgust. After walking for several hours, they had arrived at a line of wooden crosses pieced together in the shape of X's that stretched across the horizon like grave markers as far as the eye could see.

To their right, a tattered gray cloak and a tall blue hat

hung at the tips of a single cross. At the point where the wooden beams met, a grave epitaph was posted. It read,

HE WANDERS NO MORE

To their left, a moth-eaten space suit with a green dragon crest was draped over a cross. Its sign read,

THE ENDER ENDED.
THEY NOW SPEAK FOR HIM.

A small, soiled dress hung on the cross directly before them. Playing cards fluttered around it in an unnatural breeze. At its base lay a shattered mirror and an empty bottle with a tag reading *drink me*. Chance picked up the bottle and looked at the cross's sign. It read,

THE MANX FOE SHE FOUND

Chance looked down at the bottle and gasped as hordes of insects swarmed out of it and rushed over his hand. He flung the bottle to the ground and frantically brushed the bugs off him.

Chance walked down the line, Viz and the Outlaws following him as they passed crosses mounted with mouse-sized spears, rusted tin arms, fly-swarmed rabbit skins, broken swords, and every macabre talisman imaginable. Like the first three, each cross bore its own special cryptic message, every one of them alluding to some calamitous end.

At last, they came to a particularly disturbing cross. A pair of shattered spectacles, a broken broom, and a splintered wand were mounted on its crossbeams. Its message simply read,

THE BOY WHO SURVIVED, ALMOST

"What is this place?" SC asked.

"A warning," Viz said, her voice solemn, "to any would-be heroes or trespassers. These crosses mark the beginning of the wastelands. To pass beyond is to invade the Shadow Prince's territory. If you have second thoughts, now is the time to—"

Chance stepped between a pair of crosses into the wastelands and kept on going. He did not look back to see if the others followed.

13

Having other business to attend to, the Shadow Prince left Psy-chick to wander alone through the uppermost parts of Shadow Tower. As she searched for her friends through its unimaginably long corridors, she found that all doors were open to her.

I am the key after all, she thought with a smirk.

Along with more rooms of luxurious furnishings, she found rooms of unique curiosities and others that defied description altogether.

Psy-chick opened the door to one room to find a vast violet ocean that stretched as far as her eyes could see. In another, she encountered a gathering of every timepiece imaginable, all of its cuckoos, chimes, and alarms going off at once.

She walked in another that was literally upside down, with floor and ceiling juxtaposed so that furniture hung down instead of lights and chandeliers. She looked on in amazement as the leaky ceiling at her feet dripped water upward to the floor above.

"What is this place?" Believing herself alone, she was shocked to hear a reply.

"The Tower is the Prince and the Prince is the Tower. *Ribbit.*"

Psy-chick spun around to see a small, disfigured boy dressed in filthy rags gaping up at her. His spotted, green skin was covered with warts. The flesh at his neck expanded and contracted like that of a bullfrog with each breath. Startled by her sudden movement, he leaped against the wall and covered his ugly face with hands that were webbed.

"No! No! *Ribbit. Ribbit,*" the toad-boy cried. "Please no hurt Ribbit! Ribbit sorry! Ribbit sorry!"

Looking at the miserable creature, Psy-chick felt pity for it. "It's all right." She began to place her hand on the toad-boy's shoulder but pulled back when he cried out. "I'm not going to hurt you."

"Ribbit didn't mean! Ribbit be good! *Ribbit.*"

"I'm not going to hurt you," Psy-chick reiterated. "I promise."

At this, the toad-boy, who by now Psy-chick was certain called himself Ribbit, dared to peek out from behind his hands. "Promise no hurt Ribbit?"

Psy-chick smiled and drew an X on her chest with her finger. "Cross my heart."

"Pretty Girl no hurt Ribbit," Ribbit said for his own benefit as he lowered his hands. He came out of his squat into a crouch, which appeared to be the best Ribbit could do in the way of standing. "Pretty Girl no hurt Ribbit! *Ribbit. Ribbit.*" He began to hop about the room joyfully, saying it over and over, croaking froglike in between each sentence. "Pretty Girl no hurt Ribbit! *Ribbit.* Pretty Girl no hurt Ribbit! *Ribbit.*"

Growing annoyed, Psy-chick motioned for Ribbit to stop. He froze and cringed again as if expecting a lashing. But he quickly realized that wasn't going to be the case and hopped over and crouched beside her. "Ribbit like Pretty Girl. *Ribbit.*"

"And Pretty Girl, uh, I like you, too, Ribbit. My name is Psy-chick."

"Ribbit like Psy-chick, too, Pretty Girl," Ribbit assured her.

"No. Call me Psy-chick. That's my name."

"*Ribbit.* Okay, Pretty Girl."

Psy-chick sighed. "Tell me, Ribbit, what did you mean the Tower is the Prince?"

"The Tower is the Prince and the Prince is the Tower! *Ribbit.* One is the other and the other is the one!"

Psy-chick shook her head in frustration. "Okay, Ribbit. At least tell me this: what are you doing here?"

Ribbit's face sagged with sorrow. "Ribbit did bad thing so Ribbit punished. *Ribbit. Ribbit.* Ribbit belong to Shadow Prince now. *Ribbit.* Shadow Prince teach Ribbit lesson Ribbit never forget."

"Is anyone else here? Are there any others like you? Do you have any family or friends?"

"Ribbit have family once. *Ribbit*. They gone now. Now all Ribbit see is Shadowmen, and they no like Ribbit. *Ribbit*."

Psy-chick slowly extended her hand. "Well, I'm here now, Ribbit. And I like you. I'll be your friend."

Ribbit eyed Psy-chick's hand suspiciously. "Pretty Girl Ribbit's friend? *Ribbit*."

"Yes," Psy-chick said. "I'm your friend."

"Pretty Girl Ribbit's friend! *Ribbit*. Pretty Girl Ribbit's friend!"

"Congratulations, little froggy," the half-Chance half–Shadow Prince voice echoed throughout the room. "It seems you have found the one person capable of looking upon your ugly face without losing their lunch."

Ribbit backed against Psy-chick and clung to her leg, trembling with fear. They looked on warily as the black shadows beneath the hanging furniture gathered into a single mass and oozed down onto the ceiling at their feet. The sound of water being dumped into a bucket issued again as the black mass formed itself into Chance's likeness.

The Shadow Prince's gaze narrowed on Ribbit. "Boo!" He yelled, his voice once again full of thunder. Ribbit leaped headfirst into the wall twice in an effort to flee before finally making it through the door. The Shadow Prince shook with laughter as he watched Ribbit hop away.

"Is that how you get your kicks," Psy-chick asked before she was able to stop herself, "picking on the weak and helpless?"

The Shadow Prince's gaze hardened and Psy-chick's breath caught in her throat.

"I am the Shadow Prince. It honors my subjects to pay them notice of any kind." Mordred relaxed and waved off the entire affair and Psy-chick allowed herself breath again. "But I was only having a little fun with the cur."

"He's a person," Psy-chick said, still not believing she was giving her mouth all this free reign in Mordred's presence, "and my friend. He deserves respect just like us! If you could understand that, you might have a friend or two yourself!"

The floor separating Mordred from Psy-chick contracted. In an instant, he was directly in front of her, his face mere inches from her own. His eyes darkened and a sly grin crept over his face. "Perhaps friendship is something you can teach me, Psy-chick?"

Psy-chick cringed and backed away only for Mordred to close the gap between them once again.

"But he's not like us, Psy-chick," Mordred said. "We're special, you and I."

Psy-chick gawked up at Mordred, the dark, invisible power radiating off him taking her breath away.

"Come," Mordred said, "I want to show you something." Mordred extended his hand. Feeling helpless to do anything else, Psy-chick took it. The ceiling at their feet transformed into tendrils of darkness that slithered upward and enfolded them in a cocoon of shadow. The cocoon sank through the ceiling, taking them down into some new dark unknown.

14

"Run!" Viz screamed.

Chance didn't have to be told twice. He, Shocker, and Space Cadet turned from the fast-approaching sandstorm that stretched across the horizon and made a beeline for the ruins that lay roughly two hundred yards across the dunes ahead of them.

The nearing storm howled like a thousand trains blasting by at once. Chance quickened his pace as he imagined those sand-filled winds scouring the flesh from his bones in a matter of seconds. But he and the others weren't fast enough. The storm engulfed them and the safety-heralding ruins disappeared from his field of vision.

As the sand pelted against his Morlock cloak, his Burlington-made smart-mask dropped over his mouth and chin while activating a pair of lenses to shield his eyes. Two small, thin breathing tubes wormed their way beneath his face-cover, traveling from his collar over his ears to plug themselves into his nostrils.

Thank goodness for clothes-tech, Chance thought. *But this still—*

Chance spun left, barely dodging a scissoring mandible of sharp, jagged teeth as it leaped out of the sand directly in front of him. As the mouth passed, time seemed to slow so that Chance's eyes were able to take in the beast that followed in great detail. It had the head of an insect followed by the body and fins of a great shark and was covered entirely in gray-black crocodile scales. It was truly the stuff of nightmares.

Chance turned his head to see the airborne creature plunge beneath the dunes like a flying fish returning to water. His eyes widened in horror to see two more leap out of the sand toward him, their mandibles spread wide.

Just then, out of nowhere, Viz dropped out of the sand-filled sky and planted her heels in one of the beast's backs, sending it crashing to the earth as she swatted its twin out of the air with her bo staff.

Chance caught her as she tumbled clumsily from the back of the felled monster. Her striking of the other had cost Viz her footing. Both monsters dived beneath the ground, shrieking as they went.

Viz yelled something through the scarf she'd pulled over her nose and mouth for protection from the storm. Her words came out as a muffled cry, but Chance understood what she'd said well enough: sand-sharks. And by the look of it, they were in a feeding frenzy.

Viz took Chance's hand and dragged him through the storm. The sand-sharks chased after them, plunging in and out of the dunes all around them as they ran. His forearm clasped to hers, Chance swung Viz around, using her boot heels as dual clubs to knock away the beasts.

When that didn't work, they flipped and rolled over and under the leaping sharks while they beat them away with staff, clubs, and fists. Somewhere in the back of Chance's mind, he spared a second to think about how well Viz and he worked as a fighting team.

Viz pointed upward with her thumb and Chance reacted immediately, leaping as high and as far as he could. Viz joined him and they landed shoulder to shoulder in a sandstone ditch big enough to hide their crouched bodies from the storm and its sharks.

Chance watched as several of the black beasts vaulted the wall above them. Chance thought he even felt a few dull thuds through the stone of what had to be sand-sharks crashing into the wall at their backs. But the stone ditch held and it wasn't long before the storm and its sand-sharks were hurtling away.

With the winds dying down, Chance's smart mask retracted. "Good thing you know the terrain. This ditch saved our bacon! Thanks!"

"I owed you," Viz said as she removed the scarf from her face.

"Yes, you did," Chance said, grinning. "You know, we made a pretty good team back there."

"Yes." Now it was Viz who grinned. "We did."

They stared at each other for a moment and then looked away, both of them embarrassed.

"Any luck finding our friends down in that ditch?"

Chance looked up to see Shocker and SC looking down at them from above. "Uh, no."

"Well," Shocker said, "I guess we should be moving along then, huh?"

"And here I thought I was team captain!" Chance said with a smile. He and Viz got to their feet, dusted themselves off, then climbed out of the ditch.

The Outlaws walked the rest of the way to the ruins in silence. The ruins were ancient Grecian in style and the complete skeleton of what had to have once been a large, vibrant city still remained. Chance had expected to see the rubble of olden temples and statues, and of that, there was plenty. But he was shocked to also see the wreckage of World War II airplanes, eighteenth-century galleons, and countless other Earth vessels lying among the ruins.

Chance bolted toward one of the airplanes, a rusted-out American bomber he thought by the look of it, and hopped onto the wing so he could peer into the cockpit. He jerked back when he saw the skull of a long-dead airman peering out at him.

Chance heard the others approach from behind. "What is it, Chance?" SC asked.

Gathering his courage, Chance looked back into the cockpit and read the name stitched across the pilot's uniform. "It can't be," Chance said. "This plane was lost at sea in World War Two!"

"Can't be what, Chance?" Shocker asked.

Chance hoped off the plane and ran toward one of the large, beached galleons. The others jogged up to him and he grabbed for Viz's bo staff. She resisted at first, but then let him have it. Chance used the staff to knock away dirt and corrosion from the ship's busted hull. After a few minutes of knocking and scraping, a painted name appeared from beneath the grime—*Mary Celeste*.

"It's just not possible," Chance said. "This ship went down in the Atlantic Ocean centuries ago. But here it is!"

"Here what is, Chance?" Viz asked.

Chance took off again, this time for the ruins themselves. He reached a crumbling wall and used his hand to wipe away layers of sand. Strange letters and symbols were scratched faintly into the surface where he had cleaned.

Chance stared at them long and hard and then began to laugh uncontrollably.

"What the hurl's this all about, Hicksville?" Shocker asked. "What's that say?"

"It's the language of the Old Ones," Viz said, "or at least a crude version of it."

"It's ancient Greek," Chance said, wiping tears of laughter from his eyes.

"Is it the Code?" Viz asked.

That sent Chance into guffaws all over again. "For your sake, I hope not!"

"What does it say, Chance?" SC asked.

Chance quieted, though a new bout of laughter threatened to burst from him at any second. "It reads, 'Plato was here.'" That's all it took. Chance was rolling once again.

"All right, Hicksville," Shocker said. "Enough already. What gives?"

"Don't you see?" Chance said, gathering himself. "Don't you know where we are?" Chance gestured to the ruins surrounding them. "This is the lost city of Atlantis! And those planes are the ill-fated Flight Nineteen from World War Two. They were doing a routine exercise over the Bermuda Triangle when they vanished from existence!"

Shocker and SC's eyes widened.

"And that ship . . ." Chance continued, "the *Mary Celeste*—yet another victim of the triangle, as I'm sure everything else out here is."

"I don't understand," Shocker said. "What are they doing here in the Shadow Zone?"

Chance shook his head. "There must be a one-way door to the Shadow Zone somewhere in the Atlantic Ocean—someplace where the barrier between dimensions is thin enough so things can drop in, but can't get out."

SC's face darkened. "Just like us."

Chance and Shocker looked at each other, their own faces sullen.

"Almost sundown," Viz said as she watched the partially eclipsed sun sink below the horizon. The clouds had parted just in time for nightfall. "These ruins have catacombs that lead into the caves belowground. I suggest we make for them. *Fast.*"

Chance nodded. He and the Outlaws followed, heads down, as Viz led them beneath the earth.

15

Psy-chick had the sensation of movement, of traveling downward, but there were no true signs of motion within the cocoon of shadow.

"Are we going to see my friends?" she asked.

"In time," Mordred said, his tone dismissive. "For now, humor your gracious host."

Psy-chick sighed. She turned from Mordred and watched the cocoon's swirling blackness in the dim red light given off by his eyes. It was hypnotizing. When their downward journey began, she'd found it revolting and had taken great care not to come in contact with the slinking ichor. But after a time, her aversion lessened and she found herself gazing at it for long periods.

Psy-chick sensed the cocoon stop its descent. The cocoon opened and she screamed at the sight of a great red dragon standing in the cavernous room before them.

The dragon's immense bulk rose to near three stories in height. Ominous black horns sprouted from its massive head and jaw in every direction. It raked at the floor with obsidian claws the size of spears. Its crimson scaled muzzle drew back to reveal rows of glistening, yellow fangs, and its saliva left scorch marks where it dripped on the floor.

The monster roared and spread a pair of leathery wings that filled the room. The beast was held somewhat in check by two enormous chains that fastened its long, dinosaur neck to two giant stone pillars.

Out of instinct, Psy-chick recoiled and pressed herself against Mordred's side. He wrapped a reassuring arm around her shoulder. Psy-chick shrieked as a link in one of the chains snapped under the strain of the dragon's struggles. The dragon roared in triumph. It shifted its weight to better tug against the remaining chain.

"He's going to escape!" Psy-chick shouted. "We have to get out of here! He's going to—"

Psy-chick screamed as the remaining chain gave way. The dragon turned on them and charged. It roared as it opened its enormous mouth. Psy-chick's life passed before her eyes as blue fire rose in the dragon's gullet. She tried to run but Mordred held her tight.

"Are you crazy?" Psy-chick yelled as she struggled in Mordred's grasp. "It's going to torch us!"

Just as the dragon was about to envelope them in flames, Mordred's eyes flashed green and he uttered a single word that echoed with thunder. "Sleep."

The dragon dropped in its tracks directly in front of them,

unconscious, its monstrous snores reverberating off the walls of the cavernous room that was its cage.

Psy-chick finally shoved herself away from Mordred. "You todak!" Psy-chick fumed. "That thing almost killed us!"

"But it didn't," Mordred said, smiling with Chance's crooked grin. "You were never in any danger, Psy-chick. I wouldn't have let it harm you. I need you, after all."

"Oh to hurl with you!" Psy-chick retorted, clearly still angry with Mordred. But she couldn't keep her eyes or her thoughts off the dragon. It reminded her of Dracomon, the only dragon she'd ever seen until now.

Psy-chick had taken control of Dracomon's mind in the Outlaws' first true team battle at Burlington Academy. She had shared the beast's thoughts—and its strength. The sheer feral power of it had been intoxicating.

"Go ahead," Mordred said. "You know you want to."

Psy-chick startled at his words, embarrassed. She'd been gaping at the dragon like a five-year-old staring at unopened Christmas presents.

Mordred's eyes flashed and the floor separating her from the dragon drew in upon itself, bringing her to the dragon's side. The warmth radiating off the mythic beast brought a film of sweat to her skin. Psy-chick watched, transfixed as the dragon's bus-sized back rose and fell in time with its breathing. She reached out and ran her hands along its large scales. They showed like iridescent red pearls in the room's light.

"It's glorious," she whispered. "So beautiful. So deadly."

Before she knew what she was doing, Psy-chick pressed her body up against the dragon's hide. She closed her eyes, rising and falling as the beast drew breath, allowing the lethal majesty of the creature to consume her totally.

"This dragon is indigenous to the Shadow Zone." Mordred's whispers came to Psy-chick as though from far away in a dream. "The peoples who ruled here before my coming hunted them almost to extinction. Can you believe anyone would ever want to harm a creature as magnificent as this?"

Psy-chick slowly shook her head, only half-paying attention.

"Now this great red one is the last of its species," Mordred said. "I have my Shadowmen scouring the planet to find another, but I fear my efforts may be in vane."

Mordred sighed. "Do you suppose there might possibly be another dragon out there somewhere—one of its own kind to dance among the clouds with?"

"I certainly hope so," Psy-chick said dreamily. She stretched her arms out to rest on the sleeping dragon's side.

The Shadow Prince smiled.

16

Using a jar of beetles to light their way, Viz led the Outlaws through a labyrinth of underground corridors until they reached a circular shrine room. The shrine served as a hub for six branching tunnels. Nine-foot-tall statues of minotaurs stood guard at each entrance. An altar sat in the room's center. The shining beetles where everywhere, making trails in the dust as they crawled along the floor, ceiling, and walls.

"Viz," Chance said as he watched the beetles scurry, "why don't the Shadowmen come into the caves? The deep ones, I mean."

Viz shrugged. "No one knows. They just don't."

"So you've never seen any lurking about in the tunnels? Even after nightfall."

"No. Never. Why do you ask?"

Chance stroked his chin. "I'd rather not say until I've had

a chance to test a hypothesis. But I think we might all be wise to keep a jar of beetles on us at all times, aboveground or below."

Chance continued his survey of the area. Viz approached the altar and held up the jar so that Chance was able to see in detail a painting of the sun that spanned the room's ceiling.

"Sun worshippers," Chance said.

"Maybe," Viz said. "If they were anything like the Old Ones, they would've regarded light and love above all."

Chance turned to see Shocker collapse at the feet of one of the great stone minotaurs. After their trek and the excitement with the sand-sharks, he was exhausted.

"We should make camp," he said to Viz. "Have a bite to eat and then grab a few hours shut-eye before heading out again."

"We'd have to stop soon, anyway," Viz said. "And this is as good a place as any."

Shocker sighed with relief as Chance, Viz, and SC removed their cloaks and dropped their packs on the dusty floor.

"Back in a minute," SC said.

"Again?" Shocker asked.

"Hey," SC said. "What can I say? The gilly weed goes right through me."

Shocker watched SC exit the room. He sat up, wiped his face, and then got to his feet. "What I wouldn't give for some good, old-fashioned Burlington tap water," he said as he approached the altar. He removed his cloak and pack, setting the latter on top of the altar.

"No! Even better," Shocker said, "a Megalopolis chili dog!"

"I can do without Burlington's hot-dog-flavored pellets," Chance said.

"Nah, Chance," Shocker said. "I'm talking real Megalopolis cuisine. Not that soylent stuff they feed us at school.

"Back when I ran with the Irregulars, we'd go down to Mythica Park and clean out the change from the ride seat cushions. We'd always take some of the scratch and buy a whole boatload of chili dogs from this guy who had a stand next to the Xenozoic Zoo."

"Why didn't you just take the chili dogs?" Viz asked. "Here in the Shadow Zone, food goes to those bold enough to seize it!"

"Hey," Shocker said, "that guy wasn't any mere hot-dog vendor. He provided a true public service! No way I'd have ever stolen from him!"

Shocker turned back toward Chance. "Anyway, I'm telling you, Hicksville, they were the best chili dogs in the world!"

"Sounds like it."

"I'm telling you, they were."

Shocker reached inside his pack and pulled out a ball of waxy wrapping paper. He peeled away the paper and grimaced at the mass of slimy green weed it housed.

"Just imagine it's one of your chili dogs," Chance said.

Shocker scowled back at him and gave him a mock salute. "Aye, aye, Cap'n."

Chance and Viz chuckled as they watched Shocker pinch his nose and take a bite out of the wet, green mass. Shocker's gorge rose twice before he was able to swallow the gilly weed down.

"What?" Shocker asked. "Tell me you like this stuff. I know it nourishes us and keeps us hydrated, but it tastes like old gym socks!"

"Oh no!" Viz said, all sense of mirth gone from her voice. "Take your pack off the altar!"

Viz snatched up her bo staff and spun to face one of the minotaurs. Its eyes, and those of the others, opened to stare at them with blank, luminous aqua-blue gazes. The minotaurs stirred and dust flew from their bodies.

As the statues unfolded their large stone arms, the sound of concrete blocks being dragged over one another echoed throughout the shrine. But that was not the worst of it. Each minotaur brandished either a menacing scythe, short-sword, or hammer in either hand.

This is like a Ray Harryhausen nightmare come to life! Chance thought.

Terrified, Shocker jerked his pack off the altar. If it made a difference to the minotaurs, they didn't show it. They attacked from every side all at once.

Chance backflipped out of the way of a down-swiping scythe and then rolled left to dodge a stabbing short-sword. Viz tried to match weapons with the two minotaurs facing her, but was swatted backward mercilessly by the minotaurs' superior power. Shocker jumped out of the way of a hammer that came crashing down to smash the altar in his wake.

Chance, Viz, and even Shocker fought with everything they had. But it amounted to nothing against the hard stone skin of the minotaurs. The steer-headed statues steadily tightened their circle around them, forcing the three teenagers to retreat until they stood back to back. There was no escape and Chance knew it.

Chance peered between two of the hulking minotaurs and caught a glimpse of SC now returned and standing bugeyed and slack-jawed at one of the room's entrances.

"Run, SC!" Chance shouted. "There's nothing you can do! Run!"

Chance cursed himself as one of the minotaurs swung around in Space Cadet's direction. SC bolted down the tunnel and out of sight. The minotaur chased after him. The other minotaurs pressed in closer, narrowing the gap left by Space Cadet's pursuer.

A loud crash that shook the shrine room sounded from SC's exit tunnel and Chance shouted in despair, knowing his friend's end had come. With one powerful stroke after another, the remaining minotaurs knocked the weapons from Chance, Viz, and Shocker's hands. Chance and his friends were scooped up so that each of them was locked in a bear hug. They screamed in agony as the minotaurs squeezed.

The screams halted as the last of their air was pressed from their lungs. Black roses bloomed before Chance's field of vision. Then suddenly the minotaurs' arms disappeared from him and he dropped to the floor. Chance inhaled as deep as he ever had and his vision cleared. He looked up to see a minotaur hurtling through the air toward him, its limbs flailing for purchase.

Chance leaped out of its way and the statue crashed

against the wall, shattering into a cloud of dust and frag-ments. Chance retraced the vanquished statue's trajectory with his eyes. He was astonished to see Space Cadet swinging another minotaur around and around with only his bare hands.

"SC!" Chance yelled, his voice full of joyful amazement.

Space Cadet released his hold on the minotaur and, like the other, it flew across the room to shatter against the wall into a hundred pieces.

"Chance," SC said, grinning ear to ear. "I'm strong! I've got Iron Maiden's strength!"

"No kidding, pud!" Shocker said. "Now mop the floor with these blockheads!"

"Right!" SC said as he gave Shocker a thumbs-up. One of the minotaurs brought a hammer down over Space Cadet's head as he stood there. The weapon crumbled upon impact, covering SC in dust.

SC removed his glasses and wiped them clean. He placed them back on his nose and punched the open palm of his hand. "I am not amused."

He swatted the giant statue with the back of his hand and it tumbled head over heels across the room. The other two remaining minotaurs charged. SC caught them by their horns and smashed their heads together. Each exploded in a cloud of dust and debris. Their decapitated bodies went rigid and fell to the ground, once again lifeless.

Space Cadet turned to face Chance and the others. "Well," SC said as he clapped the dust from his hands, "I could get used to this!"

Chance's eyes widened as the minotaur that SC had back-handed got to its feet and charged his friend's flank.

"SC," Chance shouted, "look—"

Without turning around, SC popped the oncoming minotaur with the back of his fist. The force of the blow ran down the length of the minotaur's body, pulverizing every inch of stone into dust.

Chance ran out to clap SC on the back in congratulation.

Shocker turned to Viz. "Now do you believe we'll get to Shadow Tower and save our friends?"

Viz tilted her head. "I'm beginning to."

17

The next day, the shifting dunes of Atlantis gave way to solid ground. But the enjoyment of feeling firm earth beneath their feet was short-lived. An hour into their journey, the clouds above darkened, swelled, and then let loose a torrent of driving rain.

"Don't drink it!" Viz yelled over the sound of the pounding rain. "And keep covered up! Your cloaks will protect you!"

Chance saw smoke rising from the rocks and dirt where the rain landed and understood Viz's warning. The rain was bloated with acid. He looked down at his cloak, relieved to see it was intact and unscathed despite the acid-rain slamming against it.

Whatever these cloaks are made of, it's strong stuff! Chance thought.

Chance thought about how the Earth's rain might have

one day turned just as harmful if not for the Brotherhood of Heroes' intervention.

By supplying Earth with new, cleaner forms of energy, the Brotherhood had prevented countless potential environmental disasters. It was almost too good to be true.

On the tail of that thought came another, one spoken inside Chance's head with the voice of his old mentor, Captain Fearless.

If it seems too good to be true, lad, then it probably is! The easy way is seldom the right one.

Oh, hush! Chance thought back to his mind's stand-in version of his mentor, which in truth was just another part of him. Viz has just turned you into a Doubting Thomas with all her crazy talk about the Brotherhood knowing things are amiss here in the Shadow Zone.

Chance waited for his mind to argue, but no response came. And that irked Chance all the more, because he knew the silence given by that piece of his mind was a smug, knowing one.

"This stinks," Shocker yelled. "Can't we go underground?"

"Not if we want to make Shadow Tower by week's end," Viz yelled.

Shocker huffed and tightened his cloak about him.

They walked in the hard rain for miles until they entered a low valley and the temperature bottomed out. There, the pelting rain became pelting sleet.

"You've got to be fragging kidding me!" Shocker swore.

"I've got this," SC yelled.

Using his hand as a knife-edge, he cracked off a large slab of rock from a nearby boulder. He held it above their heads, using the slab as a makeshift umbrella for the three of them.

After a time, the sleet turned to falling snow and Space Cadet discarded the slab, having no further need of it.

"E-e-even with the c-c-cloak," Shocker said as he shivered, "It's c-c-c-cold."

"Now," Chance said, his teeth chattering, "Sh-sh-Shocker, it ain't so b-b-ba—oh, who am I k-k-kidding. It's fr-fr-freezing out here!"

SC shrugged. Of the group, he was the only one unaffected by the near-arctic conditions. "I'd help, but it's not like I can punch something to make it better this time."

"I thought the w-w-weather back in T-t-tennessee was c-c-crazy," Chance said, "but sandst-st-storms one day and snow-storms the n-n-next? I've never s-s-seen anything like it!"

"They don't c-c-call this place the wastelands without r-r-reason!" Viz said as she rooted through the already knee-high snow with her bo staff. "But w-w-we'll warm up c-c-climbing the mountain."

"Mountain?" Chance asked. He looked to the horizon ahead of them. Even through the falling snow, he had no trouble making out the distant, black silhouette that climbed upward to disappear into the clouds.

Chance sighed. "W-w-where angels fear to t-t-tread."

As sundown neared, they entered a cave halfway up the mountainside. Chance gathered some brush from around the cave mouth and, after many, many tries, was able to get a fire going by using the survival skills Captain Fearless had taught him.

Chance smiled thinking about the time the captain had put his skills to the test by dropping him off alone in the uncharted regions of the Appalachian Mountains.

Sure, Chance thought, *I laugh about it now, but that bear almost had me!*

Of course, the captain had always been nearby, just out of view, making sure no real harm came to him, although he hadn't known it at the time.

As soon as the blaze sparked, the others immediately tossed off their gear and huddled around the fire to warm themselves.

Chance frantically tore the glove from his left hand, dying to warm the near frostbitten appendage by the fire. He removed his right glove and froze, both disgusted and horrified by what he saw.

Black ichor bubbled from the wound in his palm. Chance pushed up his shirtsleeve to see the once-blue veins of his forearm's underside now turned black.

Chance shivered and pulled his sleeve back over his arm.

"You OK, Hicksville?" Shocker called.

"I'm fine," Chance said as he hurriedly put his right glove back on. "Just a little cold." Chance joined them by the fire.

"You think we're safe here?" Chance asked.

"We're far back enough in the cave so no Shadowmen patrols would see the fire," Viz said. "We're fine."

"Good," Shocker said, "I don't think I could take another step."

"We made good time today," Viz said. "Probably cut half a day's journey from the trip."

"I don't know whether to be happy or sad about that." SC said.

"Tell me about it, pud," Shocker said.

"It's good," Chance said. "It means we're that much closer to finding the others."

"Or ending up captured along with them," Shocker said.

"Shocker!" Chance chided.

"Hey, I'm just saying what's in the back of all your minds," Shocker said, "don't forget!"

"Yeah, well," Chance said, "concentrate on what's in the front—the thoughts of how we're going to rescue them."

"Sorry, Chance. You're right. I'm just tired."

"Yeah," Chance said. A shiver ran up his right arm to echo and die in his torso. He wrapped his arms around his shoulders. "We're all tired—and cold. We better turn in early tonight and recuperate from the day's journey."

"I agree," Viz said as she blew warm air over her hands. "We have a little extra time, at any rate."

Space Cadet shrugged. Thanks to Iron Maiden's near limitless stamina, he wasn't the least bit tired. "If you guys say so. I can always sleep."

After everyone had finished warming their fronts and their backs, they smoothed out the earth around the fire and spread out their packs and cloaks to bed down.

Chance fell immediately into a fitful, dream-filled sleep.

In his dreams, Chance flew over the icy tundra they'd crossed during the day. This was not like his normal flying dreams where he was full of wonder and exhilaration at soaring hundreds of feet above the earth. Here, the act of flying was all business, a feat no more special than riding the bus or taking out the trash.

In fact, Chance didn't feel anything at all. Neither love nor joy nor anger nor hate. He was just empty. No, that wasn't right. He wasn't empty, he was *cold*. His heart was frozen and ice ran in his veins (black ice, Chance thought for no discernible reason) so that he was numb to any and all sensation.

So when he dreamed he saw young superhumans fleeing in terror across the snow beneath him, it was not with a sense of right or wrong that he swooped down and scooped them up kicking and screaming into his arms to carry them off into the night. He just did what he knew he had to do. He did what the black ichor covering his body *commanded* him to do.

Chance awoke to find himself being yanked back within the cave. Viz tackled him to the ground and threw her cloak over the both of them.

Chance started to scream at the icy pain throbbing up his right arm but Viz clamped her hand over his mouth before his yell could escape.

"In the name of the Old Ones, what are you doing?" Viz whispered. "They almost saw you!"

Chance peeked through the slit created where Viz's cloak met the ground and saw a group of Shadowmen flying through the valley below. Their shiny, obsidian bodies reflected the two large moons hanging overhead.

I was sleepwalking, Chance thought, *but that was no dream! I was out there with them, at least in my head, while they were kidnapping superhuman teens! The poison in my hand is linking my mind to that of the Shadowmen!*

Chance gritted his teeth, trying not to yell as the cold jolts from his wound surged through him. Finally, the Shadowmen left the valley and his pain abated into a dull throb.

He motioned for Viz to release him. She did and they sat up.

"You could have gotten us all captured!" Viz said, still whispering, as she gestured back to Shocker and Space Cadet. They were snoring away on their makeshift beds, oblivious to what had just occurred.

"I'm sorry," Chance said. "I must have been sleepwalking. I haven't done that since, well, ever."

"Do you think it will happen again?"

Chance shook his head. "I don't know."

Viz looked down at Chance's hand. "It's the shadow-bite, isn't it? It drew you out here to the Shadowmen. It's *turning* you."

"Turning me into what?" Chance said. Viz's words had caught him off-guard and he was unable to hide the fear in his voice.

"I don't know," Viz said. "Maybe nothing. Then again, maybe something horrible—something never encountered before.

"Normally, the infection enters through your nose and travels to your brain. That's enough to bind you to the Shadow Prince's will. But as time goes by, the poison spreads until finally you become a Shadowman just like the one who infected you.

Viz's gaze fell to Chance's hand.

"You're the first person I know of to be bitten on the hand. Maybe that's it. Or maybe it's your strength of will. Or maybe the Old Ones are protecting you. Whatever it is, so far you've been able to keep your wits and remain who you are."

Behind them, Shocker gave a roaring snore. Chance and Viz turned their heads and saw SC roll over in his sleep and throw his arm across his teammate. Shocker quieted immediately.

Chance smiled. The expression fell away as he continued his conversation with Viz.

"Viz," Chance said, "I can't endanger my friends."

"What do you mean?"

Chance sat, considering. "Maybe nothing. I think I can control it. At least for the time being. But if a time comes when I can't, I need to know I can count on you."

"Count on me for what?"

Chance's face darkened. "For whatever needs doing."

18

Psy-chick trailed behind the Shadow Prince through a long, winding dark hall within Shadow Tower. Her skin was already beginning to tingle and turn red from the slight burn the dragon's radiating heat had given her the day before.

What I wouldn't give for a little sunburn cream from the Burlington Clinic! she thought.

"Are we going to see my friends?" Psy-chick asked.

"With so many other wonders still left to see?" Mordred asked. "If you thought the dragon was something, what I have to show you next will make you forget all about them!"

Mordred abruptly turned and opened one of the doors lining the left side of the hall. He stepped aside and gestured for Psy-chick to step through.

Psy-chick strode through the door, her eyes locked on to the Shadow Prince. "I sincerely doubt tha*aaaAAAAAH!*"

Psy-chick fell through the night sky, her arms and legs flailing wildly as she screamed at the top of her lungs. She looked down to see the earth rushing up at her from hundreds of feet below.

Just when she was about to hit one of the tall red cliffs constituting the landscape, Mordred snatched her out of the air and placed her in front of him on the winged black horse he was riding.

They arched upward into the gray cotton of the clouds and Psy-chick's screams changed into joyful laughter. Mordred joined in, the low rumble of his true voice masked by the sound of Chance's chuckles.

For a moment, Psy-chick leaned into him, enjoying the feel of Chance's arm around her waist.

What are you doing, girl? she thought to herself. *This isn't Chance behind you, it's a monster!*

Psy-chick jerked forward, appalled at how easily she had allowed herself to be taken in, if only for a moment.

They spiraled downward to land at the top of a large canyon. Ribbit was there, tending to an entire heard of Pegasuses. They stood, fluttering their wings as they nibbled at the sparse shrubbery beneath the moonlight.

Mordred lowered Psy-chick to the ground and then dismounted. Psy-chick stroked the black horse's muzzle and neck. It ruffled its wings in pleasure and she forgot all about being mad at herself.

"They're amazing!" Psy-chick said. "Are they from the Shadow Zone, too?"

"No," Mordred said. "These Pegasuses are from my father's stables—a parting gift before he kicked me out."

"Your father kicked you out?"

"Yes," Mordred said, his eyes flashing. "And I hate him for it. Ribbit!"

Ribbit spun on his heels to face Mordred. He'd been trying to be as small and unnoticeable as possible. Now he stood trembling as he awaited the Shadow Prince's orders.

"Yes, master? *Ribbit.*"

"Stop hitting yourself."

"But I'm not—" Much to his horror, Ribbit punched himself in the face. This blow was followed by a second from his other hand and then another and another.

Mordred guffawed in his thunderous voice.

"Mordred," Psy-chick yelled. "Stop it! You're hurting him!"

Mordred paid her no notice. He continued laughing as Ribbit smacked himself silly.

"I said stop!" Psy-chick said as she advanced on Mordred.

"Why should I?" Mordred asked.

"Because," Psy-chick said, momentarily taken aback, "he's my friend!"

"Always friend-this, friend-that with you!" Mordred said. He waved his hand, releasing his control over Ribbit. The frog-boy collapsed upon the ground. "Tell me, what's so special about a friend?"

Psy-chick looked Mordred in the eye. "I can't explain it. It's too big for words. But if you took me to Justice, Maiden, and Gothika we could show you."

"Tell you what," Mordred said, "pick any Pegasus you want. Race me to the horizon and back, then down through this canyon to where it opens before the river, and I'll take you to see your friends."

"And if I lose?" Psy-chick asked.

"Then I would ask a small favor from you, Psy-chick." Mordred's eyes narrowed on her. "I want to see some of that untapped power you're keeping so well concealed from me."

Psy-chick gulped. She suspected—heck, she was certain—that if Mordred discovered she no longer possessed her psionic powers, he would have no further use for her. But so far, winning this race was the best chance she'd had at seeing Gothika, PJ, and Iron Maiden.

What would Chance do? Psy-chick thought. The answer was immediately apparent. She had to race Mordred. And she had to win!

"OK," Psy-chick said. "You're on!"

"Excellent!" Mordred said. He turned and mounted his winged, black stallion in a single hop. "You may take as much time as you like to practice, for all the good it will do you."

Mordred raised his hands and ichor leaped from them to form a bridle over his horse's muzzle. The horse immediately began to buck and kick beneath him. "Pardon me," Mordred said as he struggled with the reins. "Nightmare's fine on a casual ride, but it's been a while since I've raced him. It seems he also needs a refresher."

Mordred kicked his heels into Nightmare's ribs. "Up and away, you beast! Your master commands it!" The dark horse leaped into the air, flying jerkily away.

Psy-chick watched them for a moment. Then she turned and walked toward the herd of Pegasuses.

A fool's hope is better than no hope at all! She thought.

An immaculate, white stallion with wings of silver neighed hospitably at her approach. She reached up and scratched his chin.

"Aren't you a handsome fellow?" Psy-chick cooed.

"That Comet!" Ribbit said as he joined them. "Comet smart! And fastest in flock! *Ribbit.* Even faster than Nightmare! *Ribbit. Ribbit.*"

Psy-chick tilted her head, curious. "Then why didn't Mordred take him? He would seem the obvious choice."

Ribbit shook his head. "Shadow Prince tried it before, with others. *Ribbit.* But after he break them, they no good no more. *Ribbit.* Best can't be broken and stay best. *Ribbit.*"

Psy-chick stared deep into the horse's eyes. "I don't want to break you, Comet, but I do need your help. Do you understand?"

Comet snorted and nodded vigorously.

"Told you Comet smart!" Ribbit said.

Psy-chick went around to Comet's left side and stroked his flank.

I used to ride horses all over my father's vineyard back home, Psy-chick thought. *How much different can it be?*

"I'm going to climb on your back now, Comet. OK?"

The Pegasus nodded.

Ribbit went to Psy-chick, squatted, and cupped his hands to make a step for her. Seconds later, she was sitting on top of Comet, looking out over the canyon.

Here goes nothing!

Psy-chick started to kick her heels into Comet's ribs but decided against it.

"Uh, Comet," Psy-chick said, "would you be so kind as to take—"

They lifted off the ground with one powerful flap of Comet's wings. Psy-chick snagged his mane in her hands, hanging on for dear life at first, then relaxing when she saw the Pegasus wasn't going to do anything to cause her to fall.

They raced upward into the night sky until Ribbit and the other Pegasuses shrank to the size of ants on the vast landscape below.

This is real! Psy-chick thought. *This is actually happening!*

Psy-chick felt a yell of joy rise in her throat. She went with it and shouted at the top of her lungs.

"I'm flying! I'm flying!"

They whirled and swooped in the air, both horse and rider gaining confidence with each maneuver. They were in the middle of a scissor-roll when a streak of shadow rocketed by them for the horizon.

"Go!" Mordred yelled as he passed, then laughed manically.

"That dirty—! Come on, Comet! Let's get them!"

Comet responded and Psy-chick realized that, until this very moment, she hadn't known what the word *fast* really meant. The world around her became a blur. They blew by Mordred and Nightmare, banked at the horizon, and then passed the Shadow Prince and his mount again on their way back to the canyon.

"Come on, Comet!" Psy-chick yelled. "Almost there!"

Psy-chick spared a glance over her shoulder. Mordred and Nightmare followed several hundred yards behind them.

Psy-chick turned her gaze forward and tightened her grip on Comet's mane. She looked down and saw Ribbit on a canyon ridge in the distance. He waved excitedly as he jumped up and down.

That's the home stretch, Psy-chick thought. "Dive, boy! Dive!"

Comet furled his wings and leaned forward. He and Psy-chick plummeted toward the canyon. They buzzed by Ribbit. The wind rushing in to fill the vacuum left in their wake almost tore Ribbit's clothes from his body.

Comet spread his wings just as they were about to hit the ground and they leveled off. Psy-chick gently tugged on Comet's mane, only needing to use the slightest touch to guide the Pegasus around, over, and under the rock formations lining the canyon floor.

Then Psy-chick's eyes grew large and Comet whinnied as flocks of shrieking harpies left their perches along the canyon walls to attack them.

The harpies had large, vulture bodies. The face of a haggish, old woman sat at the end of each of their long, crooked necks. Their mouths were filled with fangs and the sharp talons at the end of their feet glistened in the light of the Shadow Zone's twin moons.

Psy-chick ducked her head but urged Comet forward. The Pegasus swooped and rolled, barely dodging several head-on collisions with the creatures.

Two harpies flew abreast of their left flank and began snipping at Comet's legs. Psy-chick kicked the closest harpy hard with her sandaled foot. The monster banged into the harpy flying beside it and then both crashed into the canyon wall.

Psy-chick heard a shrill caw behind her. She screamed in pain as a harpy crashed into her back. The creature beat and scratched at Psy-chick with its wings and talons.

Fighting to stay on Comet's back, Psy-chick steered him toward a rock formation shaped like a giant O. They plunged through just beneath the formation's crest. There was enough room for Psy-chick and Comet's passage, but not that of the harpy. It smacked the rocks with a thud and spiraled to the canyon floor.

Psy-chick looked ahead and her heart swelled as the canyon exit, the agreed upon finish line in her and Mordred's race, came into view.

A terrified scream cut through the air. Psy-chick turned to see the harpies flying off with Ribbit held tight in their claws. Feeling torn, Psy-chick looked back at the canyon's exit.

But only for a moment.

She gritted her teeth and pulled lightly on Comet's mane, turning them around. As they did, Mordred and Nightmare blew by them, heading dead on for the canyon exit.

Paying the Shadow Prince no consideration, Psy-chick and Comet flew like a shooting star toward Ribbit and sent the harpies along the flock's rear spinning as they passed. Comet dived and then leveled off just beneath Ribbit. Psy-chick clucked her tongue and they shot upward, moving so fast the wind drew tears from Psy-chick's eyes. They hit the flock like a bullet through butter. Psy-chick snatched Ribbit from the harpies' clutches and swung him around on Comet's back so that he sat behind her.

They continued their climb until they breached the canyon for the open night sky. The harpies did not follow. Apparently the wide open spaces above the canyon weren't to their liking.

Psy-chick did not bother steering Comet back into the canyon. They flew lazily through the air toward the race's finish line. Mordred and his Pegasus were waiting on them, just as Psy-chick knew they would be.

They flew down and landed beside them on the banks of the river that emptied out of the canyon.

"You are a natural, Psy-chick," Mordred said. "I've never seen anyone take to riding a Pegasus so well on their first flight. I am very impressed!"

"I should've won!" Psy-chick said as she dismounted Comet. "And you know it!"

Ribbit slid out from behind her and led both horses away.

"You agreed to take me to my friends if I won." Psy-chick said.

"But you didn't," Mordred said.

"I couldn't leave Ribbit to the harpies."

"Couldn't you? I would have."

"And that's why he's my friend and not yours!"

"Yes. As I've said, you're going to have to teach me more about this thing called friendship. I think it must be very powerful indeed judging by the way you go on and on about seeing those you arrived with."

"More than you'll ever know. Now, please, let me see them."

"That wasn't the agreement, Psy-chick. We've covered that already."

"You're not being fair!"

"Who ever said life was fair?"

Psy-chick scowled and balled her hands into fists. She spun on her heels to face away from Mordred so that he couldn't see the tears leaking from her eyes.

She heard him approach and then jerked away when he tried to place a hand on her shoulder.

"You will see your friends in time, Psy-chick. I promise."

"Well, why not now?"

"Because you lost and so now you have something to do. The agreement was, if I won, which I did, you would give me a demonstration of your powers."

Psy-chick's breath caught in her throat.

Think fast, girl!

She turned to face Mordred. "Uh-uh. You didn't say anything about the harpies. I never would've agreed to the race if you'd told me about them. All bets are off, Mordred."

Psy-chick gave her sternest look, trying to sell her position. Her words hadn't sounded convincing even to her, but it was all she could come up with on the fly.

Mordred's eyes flashed with anger. His Chance-husk began to bubble and swell. *"How dare you defy me!"* Mordred's voice shook the ground.

"Ow!" Psy-chick yelled as she fell backward on the unsteady ground. She forced crocodile tears from her eyes.

Use everything at your disposal, that's what Chance always taught us.

It seemed to have the desired effect. Mordred shrank back. "It shouldn't trouble you to give me a small display of your psionic abilities," he said between gritted teeth. "You're being terribly unfair."

Psy-chick wiped her eyes and rose from the ground. "Who ever said life was fair?"

Stupid, girl! She thought as soon as the words had left her mouth. *Why are you taunting him? He was just beginning to calm down!*

Mordred's fury bloomed again. His Chance-husk swirled and writhed at its edges.

Psy-chick trembled, but held her ground. *He can't hurt you,* she told herself. *He needs you!*

"Sooner or later, you will do as I command," Mordred said, addressing Psy-chick in the same tone as he had Nightmare. "Or else!" He waved his hand and a free-standing door appeared upon the riverbank.

Mordred's Chance-husk changed into a giant geyser of ichor. It shot thirty-feet straight up into the air and then collapsed upon itself to seep into the ground and disappear.

The door was for Psy-chick's benefit after all. The Shadow Prince's dark powers allowed him to travel anywhere within his realm at will. It was beyond the Shadow Zone that his need for doors—and keys—came into play.

"We go back to Shadow Tower now? *Ribbit.*" Psy-chick looked down to see Ribbit at her elbow. She'd been so rattled by Mordred's tantrum she'd almost forgotten he was around.

Psy-chick sighed and opened the door. One of Shadow
Tower's great hallways was visible on its other side. Psy-chick
looked back and waved to Comet as he and the other Pegasuses leaped into the sky.

"Bye, Comet!" she called.

"Bye, horsy! *Ribbit.*"

Psy-chick frowned as she watched the Pegasuses disappear
over the horizon. She had felt so free riding through the sky
on Comet's back! Now the grim truth of her captivity came
crashing down on top of her all over again.

For a moment, Psy-chick considered whistling for Comet
to return.

I could just fly away, she thought.

Her mind answered her.

Fly away where? Mordred can locate you at will here
within the Shadow Zone. And even if you could escape, what
about your friends? Would you just leave them?

No, of course not.

Psy-chick sighed and stepped through the door back into
Shadow Tower, Ribbit following close behind her.

19

Once again asleep inside the cave, Chance began to dream. In the dream, he was just a kid named Josh again, back home in Littleton, Tennessee, with no thoughts of Chance Fortune or Burlington Academy. He sat on his bedroom floor playing with superhero action figures when he heard the kitchen telephone ring.

Chance was gripped by an inexplicable sense of fear at the sound. He knew he had to stop his mother from answering the phone. He jumped up and ran for the kitchen. But the hallway leading there seemed to stretch and stretch, and it felt as if he were running in quicksand.

Finally, he reached the hallway's end and took the small set of stairs leading to the main level in a single bound. He turned into the kitchen just as his mother lifted the receiver from its cradle.

Chance tried to shout a warning to her, but no sound came when he opened his mouth.

"Hello?" Chance's mother said into the phone. Then her face melted into a visage of panicked disbelief. "What?"

"It appears it was suicide, Mrs. Blevins."

Josh turned around and saw that they were no longer inside his house. The dream had taken them to the banks of the Tennessee River. A policeman, a celebrity cop from one of the many investigative crime shows, stood talking to his mother as his fellow officers used a tow truck to reel a car out of the water. Mrs. Blevins lost all sense of composure as they brought the car onto land and muddy water poured from its doors.

Chance realized where they were. He hadn't been there the day they'd pulled his dad's car out of the river, but this is what he'd always imagined the scene had looked like.

This was far from the first time he'd relived the day of his father's suicide in his dreams. But no matter how many times the dream occurred, the experience seemed brand new and unbearably horrible.

"No!" Chance said. "Not again! It can't be!"

Josh felt a hand, its flesh like rot over steel, grip his shoulder. He looked up in horror to see the wet, decayed corpse of his father smiling down at him.

"But it is!"

Chance awoke with a start. He sat up and rubbed his eyes. He looked around the cave to see Viz, Shocker, and SC still snoozing away. "Thank goodness," he whispered. "It was only a dream."

Chance dressed and went outside to relieve himself. He was shocked to look up and see the nearly eclipsed sun already high in the gray sky above.

"Crap! It's noon!"

Chance ran back inside the cave and shook the others awake. "Wake up, guys! It's noon!"

"Five more minutes, Mom," Shocker said as he rolled onto his side.

"Get up, Shocker," Chance said as he nudged his teammate's shoulder. "It's noon. We've lost half a day!"

"We may be able to make it up," Viz said.

Chance was amazed to turn and see her now wide awake and fully dressed. *How does she do that?*

"There's a river on the mountain's other side," Viz continued. "If we build a raft we can float down and cover twice the ground."

"Sounds way too easy," Shocker said as he yawned and sat up. "There has to be a catch."

"There is," Viz said. "That's why I never mentioned the river before. I'd only ever consider using it as a last-ditch effort."

"Is it poisonous like the rainwater?" Chance asked.

"No. But we'll have to sail over some very bad rapids. And I mean *very bad.*"

SC clasped his hands behind his head and frowned at the cave ceiling. "Of course."

"And once we're past them, it's said a Leviathan dwells in the depths farther on."

Shocker's eyes widened. "Leviathan?"

"An ancient sea monster so large it can supposedly swallow ten men whole."

"Sounds like another run-of-the-mill day in the Shadow Zone to me," Chance said. "Time's a wasting. Let's roll, Outlaws."

"I'm a Morlock, not an Outlaw," Viz corrected.

"We couldn't have gotten this far without you, Viz," Chance said. "You may be a Morlock, but you're an Outlaw, too, as far as we're concerned."

SC and Shocker nodded in agreement and Viz could not hide her smile.

They dressed quickly and hit the trail, taking the mountaintop at a gallop. When they crested the other side, they saw a purple river winding below at the mountain's foot.

With gravity doing most of the work, their gallop increased in speed and became an ungraceful run. They reached the bottom of the mountain and immediately set to work on building a raft. A forest of gnarled and twisted trees lined the riverbank. Space Cadet chopped down several trees and honed them into logs using only his hands. Viz and Shocker gathered vines to bind the logs while Chance carved a sterudder from a tree branch with his laser-cutter.

"Should we make paddles?" Shocker asked.

Chance eyed the swiftly flowing river. "No. The river's probably running faster than we can handle as it is.

"But if we need to later, SC can hang those incredibly strong feet of his over the side and kick for thrust."

By midafternoon they had assembled the logs and woven the vines in between them. SC added a hollowed out tree stump for the rudder's housing, and they were ready to set sail.

"I christen thee, the *Maiden Two*!" Shocker said and then feigned breaking a bottle over the raft's side. "May you hold as strong and be twice as sweet!"

"Twice as sweet as Iron Maiden?" SC said. "That's still going to be one sour raft!"

The three Outlaws broke into laughter. When they gained control of themselves, they pushed the raft out into the water and then hopped aboard. They were immediately swept up in the river's current, and it wasn't long before the first rapids appeared on the horizon.

"Where angels fear to tread." Chance took the rudder. "Everybody hold on!"

There was no steering around the rapids. The best Chance could do was steer into them and hope they were pushed on by the current before any serious damage could befall the raft.

They hit the fast-moving water and the raft free fell for several seconds before crashing back onto the river's surface in a brilliant spray that instantly soaked them to the bone.

Chance wiped the water from his face and tried to steady them. But the raft was into it now, rolling and bouncing over the rapids like a toy boat caught in hurricane waters. It was all Chance could do to keep the raft's nose pointed forward and its end pointed aft.

They hit another spot of gushing water, this one running over a boulder in the river's middle, and the raft vaulted up and over it, doing a flip in midair. Chance knew they were goners.

The Outlaws screamed as they saw the water replace the sky and then shouted again when they felt the raft finish the turn to smack down on the water once again.

They hit the river spinning and Chance felt his last meal of gilly weed rise into his throat. He gasped at the sight of several large rocks protruding from the water ahead of him. He fought with the rudder, trying to regain control of the raft, but to no avail.

They slammed into one rock after another, moving down the river like a pinball among flippers. But the raft held.

Finally, the river calmed and the four of them breathed a collective sigh of relief.

"I think we're going to make it!" Space Cadet said.

Shocker cocked his head to the side, listening. "Hey, what's that noise? It sounds like—"

Chance looked ahead to see the river simply vanish twenty yards ahead of them.

"Paddle!" Chance screamed. "Paddle with all you've got!"

But it was too late. Their hands weren't even in the water before they went over the roaring falls that cascaded down into a valley hundreds of feet below.

Chance's feet left the raft. His arms and legs flailed, attempting to swim in midair. But that attempt ended the same way all the ones before it had. At the last second, he gulped a breath of air, straightened his body, and splashed down through the surface of the river.

Seconds passed and Chance stopped sinking. He opened his eyes and looked around, amazed to still be alive. Chance saw Shocker's limp body ahead and swam hurriedly toward him, kicking his feet hard and fast.

Chance hooked Shocker's neck with his arm and swam for the raft. SC was there crawling on his hands and knees. He reached down and helped Chance bring Shocker aboard and lay him on his back.

"Just when you thought it was safe to go into the water," Shocker said and Chance knew he was going to be okay.

"Where's Viz?" Chance asked SC.

"Haven't seen her."

That was all Chance needed to hear. He dived into the water, frantically scanning the depths for Viz. He had to surface once for air. He was about to come up again when he spotted her, her cloak caught on the wreck of a sailing vessel unlike any Chance had ever seen.

He scooped her into his arms and headed for the surface as fast as his legs would kick. They broke through and Chance slung her onto the raft.

He pulled himself up and turned Viz's lifeless body so that she lay on her back. He began mouth-to-mouth resuscitation.

"Is she going to make it?" Space Cadet asked, clearly shaken himself.

Shocker flopped onto his belly beside them and grabbed hold of Viz's hand.

"Come on, girl!" Shocker shouted. "I know you're still in there! I can hear you!"

"Guys," SC said. "I think—"

"I don't give a flarn how hard it is," Shocker said. "You pull yourself up!"

Chance was leaning down to start again when water spewed from Viz's mouth. She coughed and they turned her onto her side so her lungs could drain.

When Viz was able, she propped herself up on her elbow and threw an arm around Shocker's neck.

"I heard," Viz gasped. "I heard you calling. You saved me. Both of you. Thank the Old Ones for you, you saved me."

Shocker smiled. "Outlaws take care of their own. That's what families do."

20

Psy-chick sat across her suite's dinner table from Ribbit, picking at the banquet spread out before them.

"You're certain you don't know where they could be?" Psy-chick asked as she plucked a single grape and popped it into her mouth.

Ribbit sat with his face submerged in his plate, showing the worst of table manners as he bit, chewed, slurped, and swallowed his way through pile after pile of food.

"Ribbit?" Psy-chick asked as she swallowed the grape. "Ribbit, I asked you a question."

Ribbit raised his head and let out an enormous belch. Food was smeared around his mouth. *"Ribbit?"*

"I asked if you were certain you didn't know where my friends are?"

"Nope. *Ribbit.* Ribbit certain. Pretty Girl Ribbit's friend.

Ribbit tell Pretty Girl if Ribbit knew." Ribbit opened his mouth and let his face fall back into his plate.

Psy-chick sighed and tried to stab the few peas rolling around on her plate with her fork. When, after several attempts, the peas remained victorious and whole, she dropped her fork and pushed her food away.

"The problem is, there are so many rooms," Psy-chick said. "We've spent the better part of the past two days opening doors in the hallways and we've not even covered this floor, much less the entire tower."

Ribbit reached for an oversized turkey leg. "Too many rooms. *Ribbit.*"

Psy-chick lowered her voice, speaking mostly to herself. "If only I still had my powers. Then I could track them down by homing in on their thoughts."

Psy-chick rolled her eyes and crossed her arms. "Ah! Where's Chance when you need him? He'd put that brain of his to work and figure out where they were in no time!"

The words were out of Psy-chick's mouth before she realized what she was saying. Tears swelled within her eyes and her bottom lip began to quiver.

Ribbit looked up from his food.

"Pretty Girl?" Ribbit asked, his voice full of concern. "Why Pretty Girl stop talking? *Ribbit.* Pretty Girl always talking. Pretty Girl never shut up. Ribbit worry when Pretty Girl not talk."

Psy-chick chuckled in spite of herself. Ribbit's clueless, innocent slight was exactly what she needed to regain control of her emotions. Losing it wouldn't do her or her friends any good right now.

"Thanks, Ribbit."

"Pretty Girl welcome. *Ribbit.* What Ribbit do?"

"Nothing, Ribbit. I'm fine."

Ribbit shrugged and dived back into his plate. Psy-chick leaned back in her chair, put her hands behind her head, and looked up at the ceiling in thought.

"Now, if I were a near-omnipotent tyrant prince wanting to hide prisoners from a houseguest, where would I keep them?"

"Underground," Ribbit said between swallows.

"Pardon?" Psy-chick asked. Her eyes snapped forward and locked on to Ribbit. "What did you say, Ribbit?"

"Ribbit say, 'Underground.' *Ribbit.* Ribbit always bury his precious to keep Sister from finding it when Ribbit little. That way, Sister no tear precious up."

Psy-chick perked up, considering. "Ribbit, I think you may be on to something there!"

"*Ribbit?*" Ribbit asked.

"The basement!" Psy-chick said. "I'll bet Mordred's hiding my friends in the basement. Or at least what passes for a basement here in Shadow Tower. Come on!"

Psy-chick bolted from the room. Ribbit took a few hurried last bites and then filled his pockets before following. They reached a spiraling, metal staircase that had what looked like black leg bones for spindles and began to descend.

Hours later, they reached the bottom and entered a sparsely illuminated hallway that was cathedral-like in size and scope. Rows of double doors ran down either side of the corridor until it terminated into an even larger set of doors guarded by a single Shadowman.

Bingo! Psy-chick thought.

She yanked Ribbit back into the stairwell before they could be spotted.

"*Ribbit!*" Ribbit protested.

"What do you want to bet the room mister tall, dark, and gruesome down there is guarding is where my friends are?"

"How will Pretty Girl get past him? *Ribbit.*"

Psy-chick smiled and batted her eyelashes. "I'll need a diversion, Ribbit."

Ribbit gave her a clumsy salute. "Ribbit help!"

"You're sure you don't mind? It could be dangerous. I wouldn't ask, but I really don't know what else to do."

"Ribbit no mind! *Ribbit, Ribbit.* Ribbit Pretty Girl's friend!"

"Oh, thank you, Ribbit!" Psy-chick smiled and hugged Ribbit. When she released him he leaped into the hallway, fluttering cartoon hearts practically hovering in the air around him.

Psy-chick peeked through the slightly parted doors as Ribbit hopped down the hallway at great speed, making his favorite noise as loudly as possible the whole way.

"*Ribbit! Ribbit! Ribbit!*"

The Shadowman's eyes flashed in warning at Ribbit's approach. When Ribbit failed to halt his advance, the Shadowman sent red eye-beams lasering toward him. Showcasing ample agility, Ribbit hopped and rolled off the floor and walls, dodging the eye-lasers.

Before the Shadowman could react, Ribbit was at him. He leaped from the floor and caught the Shadowman square in his chest with both of his webbed feet. The Shadowman was undaunted by the maneuver.

Ribbit rebounded off of him and backflipped onto the floor. He leaped out of the way of another barrage of eye-lasers and crashed through a pair of doors along the corridor wall. The Shadowman ran through the doors after him.

Seeing that he'd taken the bait, Psy-chick burst out of the stairwell and sprinted down the hallway, praying the large set of doors at the other end would not be locked.

They were not.

She reached the doors and flung them open with surprising ease. But this was the home of the Shadow Prince, after all. Why would he need to lock any doors? No one would dare to come here and attack him. The guard's presence had probably been little more than a formality left over from a time when there were those in this dimension who could actually oppose Mordred.

Psy-chick looked up and gasped at what she saw. It was not her friends before her, but a great, beating black heart suspended inside a theater-sized room. Clear tubes of plastic and steel ran from it like gigantic veins and arteries. Each coursed with gallons upon gallons of the familiar black ooze Psy-chick now realized was the literal life's blood of Shadow Tower.

Psy-chick felt someone seize her arm. She was whirled around to peer directly into the eyes of the Shadowman guard.

If Psy-chick had paused to think, what happened next

might have never occurred. But luckily for her, Psy-chick didn't think, she just reacted.

Psy-chick threw up her free hand and a bolt of electricity exploded from her arm to zap the Shadowman in his chest. He hurtled backward through the air, unconscious.

When he landed, Psy-chick noticed the ichor covering his skin had drawn away from the area where she'd hit him on the chest. For a moment, Psy-chick thought she could even hear the black ooze screaming in pain.

But Psy-chick had other more pressing things to consider at the moment. She looked down at her hands. Sparks of electricity rode up the lengths of her fingers.

"I've got Shocker's powers," she whispered in reverent awe.

After a moment, the fireworks at Psy-chick's fingertips extinguished and she turned to gaze once again at the monstrous, black heart.

Suddenly, the giant doors slammed closed. Mordred stood before her, his red eyes twinkling with rage.

Psy-chick's breath caught in her throat.

"You are never to come here again!"

Mordred waved his hand and Psy-chick found herself once again in the bedroom in which she'd awakened when first arriving at Shadow Tower.

She collapsed on the bed and sobbed into her hands.

21

"That's it for a while," Space Cadet said. "I'm bushed." He lifted his feet out of the water and crawled forward to join Shocker at the raft's head. Since they had braved the rapids, he'd been kicking up a storm at the boat's end and propelling them downriver like a guided torpedo.

"That's fine," Viz said. "We'll be somewhere we can camp soon. Then tomorrow, we'll reach Barter Town."

"Where?" Chance asked.

"Barter Town."

"What's—"

"Barter Town is one of the last cities of the Old Ones still left standing. It is one of the few places the Shadow Zone's different gangs can congregate without fear of aggression."

"How's that?" Shocker asked. "I thought all the different factions were at war with one another."

"Normally that is the case," Viz replied. "But Barter Town is sacred. It is where we all learned of the Code."

"Code this," Shocker said. "Code that! What in blue blazes is—"

"Hush!" Viz barked. She grabbed her bo staff and scanned the water, looking for some unseen threat. Chance leaped up from his place at the rudder, ready to fight.

"What gives?" Shocker said. "I was just asking—"

The raft bucked beneath them. The Outlaws were knocked off their feet. The raft bucked again and they scrambled to gain handholds wherever they could find them.

"It's the leviathan!" Viz yelled.

"Hold on!" Chance yelled.

"Like we have to be told!" Shocker yelled, when suddenly, the waters quieted and the raft stilled.

"Is he gone?" Space Cadet asked.

"We couldn't be that lucky," Shocker said. "No offense, Chance."

"None taken," Chance said. He crawled toward the raft's edge.

"Chance!" Viz called. "Be careful!"

Chance stopped and looked at her.

Chance gave Viz a reassuring wink, then proceeded to the raft's edge.

The river was murky here. He saw nothing but darkness. He didn't like it. It was too quiet—like a train station before the passenger cars came bulleting in.

Without warning, pain from Chance's shadow-bite wound shot up his right arm. He jerked back from the raft's edge just as a creature, a thing half-whale and half-serpent, burst from the water and sent the Outlaws and their raft hurtling into the air.

Chance splashed down and sank beneath the river's surface. He looked up and saw a cave of teeth slowly opening as it rushed toward him.

Chance swam for his life, though he knew the effort was a futile one. The leviathan's mouth closed around him and his purple, watery world collapsed into shadow.

Chance awoke to the sight of darkness, amazed to still be alive. The surface beneath him was squishy, and the rankest stink he'd ever smelled hung in the air. He was covered in slime. He shed his cloak. It was useless in its current state.

"Where am I?" he whispered. He rose up on all fours and took a waterproof flashlight from his utility belt. The light revealed a black, gaping skull directly in front of him. He gasped and scrambled backward.

He shined the light around, horrified to see more skeletons of all shapes and sizes lying with him in a vast chamber. He was shocked to see a half-crushed 1954 Buick Roadmaster sitting among the bones.

"How the heck did that get in here?" Chance realized he wasn't entirely sure where *here* was and shined the flashlight on the chamber walls. They were white with squiggly lines of purple and blue running all across them.

A low rumbling echoed throughout the chamber. The walls rippled before Chance's eyes as the ground moved beneath his feet and he realized the chamber was not a chamber at all.

"Well call me Jonah and slap me silly," Chance said, his jaw dropping. "I'm inside the leviathan's belly."

Chance's hand began to ache as he felt panic rise from the pit of his stomach.

"Nah, ah, ah!" he warned himself. "That won't do me any good."

I've got to figure a way out, Chance thought. *I know! I'll smoke my way out of here. If a wooden puppet can do it, then so can I!*

Chance rummaged among the bones, looking for some dry enough to burn. It was tricky work. Leviathan would unexpectedly change direction and everything within its belly, including Chance, would be tossed around like stuffed toys.

After a while, Chance realized his plan of building a fire was futile. Every bone he found was covered with slime and soaked to the core.

"Oh no," Chance said. The wet bones had put a fearful idea into his head. He took out a flare from his utility belt. His heart sank to see it covered in slime. Chance tried to light it. The flare sputtered and went out.

Maybe my laser-cutter, Chance thought, or the thermite. They'll burn just about anything. But Chance found they were covered in gunk like everything else.

Chance collapsed onto his bottom and buried his face in his hands. He didn't know what to do and he knew it meant he was going to die here.

He looked up at the first black skull he'd seen inside the leviathan's belly. Its open, rictus grin seemed to mock him.

Chance looked back at the old Buick. He was astounded to see Helix, the extradimensional imp and Burlington Academy's resident mascot, sitting in the driver's seat. The little green man was dressed in a chauffeur's uniform.

The darkness and despair must be getting to me, Chance thought. I'm delusional!

"Nothing like a Sunday afternoon drive to clear your head," Helix said.

"Helix?" Chance asked, flabbergasted. "Is that really you, or am I hallucinating?"

Helix winked. "Does it matter?" The imp gave the Buick's horn two quick honks and disappeared.

Chance stared at the empty Buick.

"No. No it doesn't matter at all!"

Chance ran over to the Buick, his feet sinking into the bottom of the leviathan's stomach with every step. He jumped in the driver's seat and was ecstatic to see the car keys in the ignition.

"Come on, baby!"

Chance turned the ignition key and began to pray. The engine sputtered, but wouldn't turn over.

"That's just fine, girl," Chance said. "Spark is all I need. Well, that and some jumper cables!"

Chance got out of the car and walked around to its trunk. He pried open the lid and shined his flashlight inside. His previously sunken heart leaped into his throat at the sight of a pair of blue jumper cables.

Chance took the cables from the trunk and then popped the hood. He walked around to the front of the car and fastened two of the cable's four sets of alligator clips to the posts protruding from the car battery. He rubbed the set of clips at the cable's other end together and sparks flew.

"Oh yeah!" Chance said. "Now to complete the circuit."

Chance dropped to his knees.

Good thing my uniform's grounded. As long as I don't make contact with my skin, this shouldn't be any problem.

"Here goes nothing!" Chance said and stuck the cable's teeth onto the squishy floor of the leviathan's belly.

The scene became instant chaos. Chance heard the leviathan roar in pain as the walls and floor of its stomach convulsed with the charge.

Chance released the leviathan from the cables.

"Oh, you didn't like that at all, did you, big boy? Quite a tender spot to have those volts coursing through, isn't it?"

Chance rolled out of the way as the Buick and just about everything else in the leviathan's stomach surged forward.

"It's working!" Chance said. "One more charge and he'll vomit us up!"

Chance battened the cables back onto the leviathan's stomach and then ran for the car as the monster's belly convulsed around him. He wrapped his fingers around the Buick's steering wheel just as the leviathan's stomach muscles pressed closed behind the car and shot them up the monster's esophagus.

Chance yelled with glee as he saw the leviathan's cavernous mouth open to reveal twilight sky. He buckled his seat belt. Then he was hurtling through the air, fear replacing the excitement in his scream.

The Buick hit the river's shore with a teeth-rattling thud. Chance unbuckled his seat belt and opened the driver's side door. He collapsed out of the Buick onto his hands and knees and kissed the brown sand beneath him.

Chance looked up to see Shocker, Viz, and Space Cadet just up the shore gazing at him, their mouths agape.

He stumbled to his feet and approached them, sparing quick glances at the river. The leviathan was no where to be seen.

"Wow, man!" Shocker said. "You hurling drove out of the thing like a hovercar racer!"

The three of them ran toward him.

"I lost my pack and cloak," Chance said.

"So did we—" The Outlaws grimaced as the wind changed direction.

"Like that?" Chance asked. "It's parfume de Leviathan!"

Viz shook her head. "Come on. Let's find us a cave."

22

The next day, Psy-chick sat alone in the fireside chair of her dining room, a look of resolution on her face.

"Mordred," she said to the room, "I want to speak to you."

What am I doing? Psy-chick thought. *I must be crazy!*

"Well? I'm waiting."

Psy-chick's wait was a short one. The room's shadows crept across the floor and gathered before her.

Too late to turn back now, she thought.

The swirling shadows lifted from the floor and began to take shape.

Don't be afraid! she thought. *Don't be afraid! Don't be—*

"It is a brave guest who summons the lord of the realm as though he were but a manservant," Mordred said as he solidified into his Chance-form.

For the first time, Psy-chick found the echoing thunder of Mordred's voice comedic rather than frightening. She imagined a baboon beating its chest and had to stop herself from snickering.

"Forgive me, my lord," Psy-chick said. "I meant no disrespect."

Psy-chick got up from her chair and knelt before the Shadow Prince, having to stifle another snicker before raising her head again.

"Well," Mordred said, obviously pleased, "consider yourself forgiven, my lady.

"To what do I owe the pleasure of your call?"

"Your father is a fool," Psy-chick said matter-of-factly.

"Pardon?"

"He did not understand your grandeur or your intelligence," Psy-chick said. "Moreover, he was threatened by it. He did not approve of someone having ideas of their own. He feared what would happen if others realized how special you are—how much more special than he is. That is why he kicked you out."

Mordred gaped at Psy-chick in wide-eyed astonishment. "How did you—?" Then a smile crept over his face. "So, you've finally decided to be reasonable and show me your powers."

If you say so, Psy-chick thought. *Never mind that practically every teenager, even one aeons-old, feels that way about their parents at one time or another!*

"I've given you a small display," Psy-chick said, "but adequate, yes?"

"Yes," Mordred said, "most adequate."

Psy-chick sighed inwardly with relief. Her gambit had worked. Mordred thought she'd read his mind.

Mordred offered Psy-chick the crook of his arm. "Let's take a walk, shall we?"

Psy-chick stood and placed her arm in his. The Shadow Prince gave her Chance's crooked smile and she once again had to remind herself that it was not her friend and captain she was standing arm-in-arm with.

But they are alike in some ways, Psy-chick thought. *Not least of all, the holes they have in their hearts where their fathers are concerned. It makes them vulnerable despite their outward shows of confidence.*

And you just used that to your advantage, Psy-chick's mind snapped back at her. How does it feel to be a creep?

"Is something the matter?" Mordred asked.

Psy-chick realized she was frowning and put on a smile. "Nothing at all, why?"

"For a moment, you seemed . . . distraught."

"Oh, it's nothing. I was just thinking about how silly I've been acting all this time."

Mordred's smile widened. "Better late than never, as you three-dimensionals say. But enough of that."

The Shadow Prince waved his free hand and an inky, black swirl appeared in the air. It rotated outward, gaining size and becoming silvery in color. The shiny mass formed itself into an oval window. Psy-chick could scarcely believe her eyes when she saw Gothika, Private Justice, and Iron Maiden chatting happily as they played cards on the window's other side.

"You're not the only one who can be reasonable," Mordred

said. "I like nothing better than to reward obedience and loyalty."

Psy-chick was speechless. She reached out to touch the window and it faded before her eyes.

"How do I know that was really them?" she asked.

"Psy-chick," Mordred said, looking abashed. "I'm hurt. And here I thought you'd decided to trust me."

Easy, girl. Psy-chick thought. *You're about to blow it! Stick to the plan.*

"You're right, Mordred," Psy-chick said. "It's time we both started acting civil toward each other."

"My thoughts exactly."

"But if I'm going to do what you ask, you've got to let me talk to them."

"I'm afraid that's quite out of the question."

"But why?"

"Because I am the Shadow Prince, and I say so." Mordred's words were punctuated by echoing thunder.

He's near omnipotent, Psy-chick thought, *but still so like a child threatening to take his ball and go home.*

"Well, then you must promise to let us go—all of us—the moment my job is done."

"But of course," Mordred said.

"Speaking of which," Psy-chick said, "you've told me you want me to rip open a hole in this dimension's barrier. But you haven't said exactly how I'm supposed to do that. I've never used my powers in such a fashion. I wouldn't even know where to begin."

Mordred waved his hand again and Psy-chick gasped as blackness enshrouded them. When the darkness retreated, Psy-chick saw they had left her bedroom and reintegrated inside what looked like a large, dome-enclosed laboratory lit only by blinking lights and panels.

A man in a black hood and cloak stood in the room's center, manipulating holographic interfaces displayed above a platform-shaped control panel. A large hologram of twin moons passing in front of a yellow dwarf sun hovered in the air above him.

"Dr. Faustoid," Mordred said to the man, "how goes your progress?"

"Master," Dr. Faustoid said as he whirled and bowed. His face remained hidden in shadow beneath his hood, but Psy-chick recognized his voice. It was Dr. Faustoid who had called her "the one" when she had arrived at Shadow Tower.

"The eclipse will be complete within two days' time," Dr. Faustoid continued. "Soon the veil separating this dimension from all others shall be rent asunder!"

"Excellent," Mordred said. "I have brought the key."

Dr. Faustoid abruptly stood and hobbled toward them. As he approached, his features became clear. His face was little more than skin stretched across a circuit board and held in place by metal pins. His eyes were like camera lenses. Psy-chick could hear a low whirring sound as their internal shutters tightened to focus in on her.

"The key!" Dr. Faustoid said, his voice taking on a digital edge.

Dr. Faustoid raised his arms and claws of black steel

reached out from beneath his cloak to touch Psy-chick. She took a step back, her eyes wide with fear and revulsion.

"That's quite far enough," Mordred scolded.

Dr. Faustoid immediately froze.

"Yes, master. Of course."

"Explain to Psy-chick how it is she will aid us in our endeavor."

"Psy-chick?" Dr. Faustoid asked.

Mordred rolled his eyes, impatient. "The key!"

"Oh! Yes! I'd be delighted!"

Dr. Faustoid returned to the control panel at the room's center. After some tinkering, he turned and spoke.

"Master, you may wish to step back for this."

Mordred nodded and stepped back among the shadows. The machine-man turned once again and manipulated a final interface. A hole opened in the room's ceiling. Psy-chick could see the nearly eclipsed sun directly above. A single shaft of its light shone down onto the control panel's platform.

We must be at the very top of Shadow Tower, Psy-chick thought.

Six large metal posts rose around the edges of the room. The dome walls began to spin on the floor, picking up speed until Psy-chick felt as if she were inside a carnival spook house. Then, green lightning shot from the posts to bounce off the rotating walls.

It's like a crude Infinity Chamber, Psy-chick thought, recalling the dimension-hopping room back at Burlington Academy.

Dr. Faustoid gestured toward the pedestal-sized control panel. "When the eclipse is complete, and the key—or rather, the *power source*—is in place, then this Vortex Chamber will tear open the fabric of space-time and allow my master's passage from the Shadow Zone!"

"And then what?" Psy-chick asked, although she was afraid she already knew the answer.

Mordred clenched his jaw and his red eyes flashed.

"And then I expand my militia of Shadowmen into an army raised from the most powerful beings in all the known worlds!"

"Yes!" The machine-man said. He clapped his metal hands giddily.

"Then we storm my father's gates and make him pay! He, and all who would stand with him!"

23

Since Mordred often left the Tower at night to hunt with his Shadowmen, Psy-chick decided to wait until then to institute the next and most crucial part of her plan to save her friends and herself from the Shadow Prince.

She didn't believe for a minute that the image Mordred had shown her had really been her friends. Now, if he'd conjured an image of them playfully bickering with one another, that she might have swallowed.

But the Shadow Prince had made a grievous error in showing them all deliriously happy and content. Sure, the Outlaws were the best of friends, but when you put teenage egos in a room together, especially superhuman ones, sparks both good and bad are bound to fly.

But if this part of her plan worked out, she'd ultimately have all the time in the world to look for her real friends.

And if it didn't, well, she wouldn't be worrying about finding them or anything else afterward.

Psy-chick led Ribbit down the same winding staircase they had traversed when they had found Shadow Tower's heart. The scent of fire and brimstone grew heavier in the air with their every step.

"It's getting hotter," Psy-chick said. "If not this floor, then the next one."

Ribbit huffed behind her, a large roasted bird the size of a small ostrich riding on his back.

"Ribbit no see why Pretty Girl wants to waste perfectly good food. *Ribbit*."

Psy-chick left the staircase to walk down a door-filled hallway. Ribbit followed.

"There will be another one waiting on us at the dinner table when we get back, Ribbit."

"How Pretty Girl know? *Ribbit*."

"There always is."

"Pretty Girl has point."

Psy-chick abruptly turned and pressed her hands against an ornate wooden door.

"Yes," she said. "It's very warm. I think this one is it."

Ribbit's knees began to knock as he looked at the door. "Ribbit scared. *Ribbit*."

Psy-chick put a hand on his shoulder.

"It's okay, Ribbit. You don't have to go inside. I'll take it from here."

"Ribbit want to help Pretty Girl, but Ribbit . . . Ribbit just can't."

"I know, Ribbit. Don't worry. You've done your job and brought the bird down here. The rest falls on me. You stay out here where it's safe."

Ribbit nodded. He unshouldered the bird, his eyes on his feet. Psy-chick took the straps she'd torn from the drapes in her room and looped them around the bird. Then she slung the bird over her back and secured it to her body with the excess straps so that she could carry it like a backpack.

Psy-chick gave Ribbit a last reassuring smile and then turned and opened the door. A breeze of extremely warm air carrying the scent of brimstone washed over her. She'd expected to see the dragon in the large room once again chained to the stone columns. But nothing of the sort met her eyes.

The mouth of a large cave stood in the open night air on the door's other side. A narrow river that was little more than a creek emptied into it. Or ran out. Psy-chick was not sure which. She could see flickering light down inside the cave's throat.

Maybe this is the wrong place? Psy-chick thought. *Maybe the dragon's not here.*

Psy-chick's gaze fell on a giant, molted dragon-skin lying just inside the cave mouth.

Nope, she thought. *This is it. Mordred must have put the dragon in the room for my benefit—his idea of a controlled environment—ha! This must be the dragon's real habitat.*

Psy-chick stepped through the doorway and it closed behind her. She turned to see the door standing on its own, attached to nothing but the horizon. Shadow Tower stood to its left, less than a mile away.

Somewhere back there, Ribbit is waiting for me on the other side of this door, Psy-chick thought, not without some wonderment.

Psy-chick looked at Shadow Tower a moment longer and then turned and followed the river into the cave. The flickering light grew stronger the farther she went in.

Psy-chick heard crunching under her feet and looked down to see bones snapping beneath her sandals.

Good heavens, I really must be insane! she thought. But she kept walking forward.

She rounded a corner and gasped when she saw three monstrous canines gnawing on the bones littered along the cave floor. But these creatures weren't dogs, exactly. Instead of fur, their bodies were covered by dark lizard scales. Their tails were forked and sharp, webbed plumage ran down the lengths of their spines.

Psy-chick immediately began to think of the monsters as wolfosaurs. She shuddered at the name her mind had formed.

The wolfosaurs sensed her fear and looked up to see who'd interrupted their dinner. Their eyes found the bird on Psy-chick's back. They looked down at the bones at their feet and then raised their heads once again, low growls issuing from their throats.

Oh crap, Psy-chick thought as the pack began to creep toward her.

Psy-chick backed against the cave, trying to protect the bird.

Steady girl, she thought. *Steady, you're not without recourse, here. You know what you've got to do. The leader will be the one out in front. Wait until he gets close—so close you can't miss!*

The largest of the three wolfosaurs eased out in front of the pack. He slowly, cautiously closed the distance between Psy-chick and himself.

He crouched down on his haunches, his fangs bared, his webbed ears pressed against the back of his scaly head.

Ready! Psy-chick thought. *Aim!*

The wolfosaur roared as it leaped into the air.

Fire!

The wolfosaur yelped as a bolt of lightning from Psy-chick's eyes caught it in midair. It flipped backward head over heels and then bounded across the river for the opposite side of the cave. It got there and kept going, making a beeline for the cave's entrance. The other two beasts whined at Psy-chick and then scampered off after their vanquished leader.

"That was a close one!" Psy-chick said as she sighed in relief.

Closer still yet to come, her mind told her.

Psy-chick followed the river inward without further incident. She was covered in sweat from the heat by the time she reached the river's source—a large underground lake inside an enormous cavern. Blue fire, the source of the cave's flickering light, inexplicably burned in patches along the lake's surface. It looked like a scene from her worst nightmares. She truly was inside the lair of the beast.

Psy-chick forced herself not to scream when the great red dragon suddenly rose out of the water in a gushing spray. The beast's eyes fixed on her. It raised its head to the cavern's ceiling and belched flames as it roared in fury at her intrusion into its lair.

The dragon snapped its massive jaws shut and climbed out onto the lakeshore. It snarled as it snaked its neck out toward Psy-chick. She reached behind her and tore a roasted leg off the bird she carried. She held it out and the beast stopped its forward progress. It cocked its head and sniffed the air.

Psy-chick hurled the bird leg into the air, tossing it with both hands like a log. The dragon snatched the roasted bird leg between its jaws and swallowed. The beast licked its scaly lips, ready for more.

Psy-chick tossed it the other leg, and then the wings. When the dragon had finished those, she dropped the rest of the bird onto the floor and stepped aside to let the dragon eat. The dragon needed no encouragement. The beast tore into the bird hard and fast.

Psy-chick crept down the dragon's length to its side. The beast didn't notice her. It was too enthralled in consuming the bird.

She reached out toward the dragon. "I hope this works like I've seen with the alligators on holovision."

Psy-chick delicately rubbed the dragon's side. At first the

beast's eyes widened in surprise. Then they closed to mere slits as the dragon relaxed to enjoy the petting. After a time, the dragon rolled over, exposing its belly to Psy-chick.

It growled with pleasure as she stroked its soft underscales.

It's working, Psy-chick thought. *Thank heaven! We may get out of this mess yet!*

24

"We're here," Viz said.

Chance scanned the area but saw only twisted trees and sparse vegetation.

"We've been walking all day, Viz," Chance said. "The sun's almost down. Now's not the time to joke. We need to get belowground, and fast."

"I'm not joking," Viz said. She stepped forward and reached her hand out into the air. Time and space rippled at her touch.

"Holy schnikees!" Space Cadet said. "How'd you do that?"

"I didn't do anything," Viz said. "Come on."

Viz stepped through the air where she had reached out her hand. The forest rippled around her and then she was gone.

Shocker shrugged. "I don't sense anything. But what the

hurl?" Shocker took a step toward where Viz had disappeared and did likewise.

"Wait for me," Space Cadet said and then he was also gone.

"Probably some kind of permeable surface," Chance whispered. "Like that of Kirby Coliseum back at Burlington Academy. But cloaked, too."

Chance gritted his teeth. "Where angels fear to tread."

Chance stepped through and the forest rippled around him. He looked up and saw that he, Viz, Shocker, and Space Cadet now stood on the outskirts of a gleaming, crystalline village. Its streets were teeming with young superhumans of all descriptions.

"This must be Barter Town," Chance said in amazement.

"That's what we call it, at least," Viz replied. "But it was built by the Old Ones. It is the last bastion of their presence on this world. Whatever the Shadow Prince's powers, he has yet to find it, though it's practically sitting on his doorstep."

"Are there any left here?" Space Cadet asked. "The Old Ones, I mean."

"No," Viz said. "No one knows what happened to them. Most, including my own gang, the Morlocks, tend to believe the Shadow Prince drove them out or killed them. But I like to think they left of their own accord long before he arrived."

"So what's this Code they left behind that you're always going on about?" Shocker asked.

Viz took a step forward and reached out her hand over the walkway. A crystal podium rose out of the ground before her.

She rearranged several smaller crystals stretching from receptacles along its top. A recorded voice filled the air.

"Even though you have been raised as a human being," the recording said, "you are not one of them. You have great powers only some of which you have, as yet, discovered—"

"Oops," Viz said. "Wrong crystal."

She swapped a green crystal for a clear one and a new recording began.

"With the blessing of power," the recording said, "comes the burden of responsibility. Treat others as you would have them treat you."

Viz stepped back and the podium sank into the ground.

Chance grinned and shook his head. "We've heard this all before, though worded a little differently. The Burlington motto is 'God makes us strong so that we may protect the weak.'"

"Of course you've heard it before," Viz said. "It's the truth!"

Chance rocked his head back as though he'd been dealt a blow and then nodded gently.

"Come," Viz said. "We need to find lodging for the night."

"And some food!" Space Cadet said. "I'm starving!"

"Surprise, surprise," Shocker said.

The three of them followed Viz into the village. She stopped and asked for room and board at several places. Each turned them away due to the Outlaws' lack of goods to trade for payment.

"What are we going to do?" Space Cadet asked.

Just then, shouts of joy and outrage sounded among a crowd gathered in the street behind them.

Chance studied them a moment and then walked over to see what was going on. The others followed him as he worked his way to the crowd's center.

Inside the boisterous gathering, two immensely large superhumans sat at a crystal table engaged in a bout of arm-wrestling. One had orange skin stretched over the biggest muscles Chance had ever seen. The other was equally thick but his skin consisted of green metal plates.

As he watched them struggle, a law of physics came to Chance's mind—the one about an immovable object meeting an irresistible force.

At last, the orange arm-wrestler began to gain ground over the green one. He inched the back of his opponent's green hand ever closer to the tabletop as the crowd shouted around them.

In a burst of speed, the orange one lifted their hands back up and then slammed them down through the table, shattering it to pieces and sending his vanquished green foe toppling out of his chair.

The crowd cheered and began to trade goods all around the Outlaws.

"They're gambling on this," Shocker said.

Space Cadet snapped his fingers. "Bet on me, Chance! I can win us the goods we need to buy lodging. I know I can!"

"It's not a bad idea," Shocker said.

The orange champion stood and began to shout. "Ooklak

and his Uruks are the strongest! Ooklak crush all comers! No gang can stand against the Uruks!"

Chance shook his head. "I don't know, SC. This guy looks like he could even take on Block. No offense, but I'm not sure Iron Maiden's strength will be enough."

SC looked his leader in the eye. "What choice do we have?"

"Ooklak have new contender?" Ooklak pointed his finger at Space Cadet. "What have you to put up against Ooklak's goods?"

"Weapons—" Shocker lied

"Shocker!" Chance spat.

"Food," Shocker continued, "and all the fresh water you can drink!"

"Ooklak agree!"

Space Cadet nodded and stepped forward. The crowd roared with approval as another table was brought out for the match. Ooklak and SC sat down and clasped hands. Another orange-skinned Uruk stepped out of the crowd and wrapped their hands together in black fabric.

"Puny fat one no cry when Ooklak break his arm."

"Go for it!" SC said.

The attending Uruk placed his hands on both of theirs and then abruptly lifted them off. "Go!"

Ooklak immediately threw his shoulder forward, adding leverage to his arm. He pushed Space Cadet's arm half the distance to the tabletop with the motion.

"Come on, pud!" Shocker shouted. "Give it to him!"

SC gritted his teeth and stopped his arm from dropping

the rest of the way. His body began to tremble as he slowly forced their arms back into an upright position and then over toward Ooklak's side of the table.

"You can do it, SC!" Viz shouted.

They went back and forth that way for several minutes, each momentarily gaining an advantage only to lose it again, the crowd going wild around them.

Chance watched in horror as Ooklak raised his foot off the ground, knowing what was about to happen, but being powerless to stop it. The Uruk brought his heel down over the bridge of Space Cadet's foot. SC yowled in pain and Ooklak slammed their hands down on the table. He stood and roared in victory.

The Outlaws stood watching crestfallen in disbelief. SC got up from the table, tears leaking from his eyes.

"I'm so sorry, Chance," Space Cadet said. "I did my best."

"I know you did, SC," Chance said as he patted his friend on the shoulder.

"Oh!" Ooklak said. "Little fat boy cry now that he lose? Go ahead little fat boy! Cry, cry! Boo-hoo!"

Fury burned within Chance, along with what felt like volts of electricity running up his arm from the shadow-bite. But it didn't hurt. In fact, it felt good—it felt powerful. In that moment, the idea that he could take Ooklak down struck him with absolute certainty.

"Because you cheated, you dirty nerfherder!" Viz screamed.

"Ooklak no cheat! Ooklak want weapons and food you promised!"

"Ooklak!" Chance growled. "Care to make it double or nothing?"

Ooklak laughed. "You sure little boy?"

"Dead sure."

"What are you doing, Chance?" Shocker asked as he grabbed Chance by the arm. "I've already got us in deep enough as it is!"

Chance shook him off and strode forward to meet Ooklak at the table, the crowd going crazy around him.

They sat down and Chance offered his right hand. Limitless power seemed to be coursing down it from the shadow-bite in waves. But Chance's eyes grew wide when Ooklak grunted in negative and offered his left arm instead of the right.

Chance shook his right arm insistently.

"No!" Ooklak's Uruks shouted. "Ooklak champion! Ooklak decide which arm!"

The crowd shouted in agreement.

Chance's heart sank and the strength that had been flowing up his right arm vanished.

What am I going to do? Chance thought. He shakily offered his left arm. Ooklak took it and the Uruk referee began to wrap their hands.

Do what I've always told you, lad, Captain Fearless's voice said inside his mind. Don't fight his fight, fight yours!

Inspiration struck and Chance grinned. He tightened the muscles in his arm and leaned forward. Ooklak also leaned forward, taking Chance's action to mean he was trying to gain position.

"What little boy grinning at?" Ooklak asked.

His face was mere inches away from Chance's own. The Uruk referee placed his hand on theirs.

"Has anyone ever told you what beautiful eyes you have, Ooklak?"

The Uruk referee lifted his hands. "Go!"

Chance leaned in and kissed Ooklak full on the mouth. Ooklak rocked back in wide-eyed surprise. Chance slammed Ooklak's hand down on the tabletop before the Uruk could regain his composure. The crowd roared equally with cheers, boos, and laughter.

Chance abruptly stood up and yanked his hand out of the wrapping and away from Ooklak's.

"I won!" Chance proclaimed. "Now give us the goods you owe!"

Ooklak stood up, knocking over the table and chairs in the process. "No! You cheat Ooklak! Ooklak will not!"

The Uruks gathered behind their leader, ready to fight.

Another superhuman in the crowd stepped forward. She was tall and lean and energy swirled in her eyes.

"Oh, yes you will," she said. "And you'll do it without argument here in the sacred city. Or would you have it said that the Uruks are welchers and violators of the Code?"

The remainder of the crowd gathered behind the girl. They were joined by passersby until they far outnumbered the gang of Uruks.

Ooklak grimaced. "Give it."

The Uruks behind him stepped forward and tossed weapons and other trinkets at the Outlaws' feet. The girl stepped back and then the crowd dissipated.

Viz, Shocker, and SC gathered the Uruks' offerings while Chance and Ooklak stared one another down. When the Outlaws finished, they turned and walked away.

"Pleasure doing business with you, Ooklak," Chance called over his shoulder. He winked and blew Ooklak a kiss.

Ooklak roared and smashed the crystal table with a single blow of his fist as he watched them go.

"Sleep with one eye open once out of Barter Town, little boy!"

25

The next day, Psy-chick was taking food off her dinner table and stuffing it in a satchel she had found in one of her many closets when she heard Mordred speak from behind her.

"Hello, Psy-chick," the Shadow Prince said.

Psy-chick momentarily froze and then turned around to face him, being sure to keep the satchel behind her back and out of Mordred's view.

"What are you doing there?" Psy-chick blinked and Mordred was beside her, taking the satchel from her hands. "Is the food I provide you served so rarely that you must store it away in a satchel for later?"

"Uh, I, that is," Psy-chick stuttered, "I was going to feed the Pegasuses."

Mordred chuckled as he pulled a large bit of roasted flesh from the satchel.

"I don't think they'd find barbecued boar meat all that appealing."

"Uh, yes, of course, uh, that's for me."

Mordred cocked an eyebrow.

"I didn't realize you three-dimensionals had such large appetites."

Psy-chick snatched the boar meat from him and stuffed it back in the satchel, thinking herself silly for taking offense. But she couldn't help it.

"So I like a big dinner? So what?"

Mordred chuckled again.

"Yes, about that. I don't have anything that needs seeing to tonight. What say we get out and catch a breath of fresh air? We could ride the Pegasus again!"

"Why, I'd like nothing better," Psy-chick lied. But she was stuck. She only hoped Mordred would tire of her company in time for her to go feed the dragon again. It was truly a brilliant animal. Psy-chick had taught it how to play all kinds of games like fetch and roll over on the first night alone. With any luck, her plans would culminate before week's end.

"All right then," Mordred said. "It's settled."

Psy-chick feigned a smile.

That night, after their ride on the Pegasuses, the two of them sat down for a late dinner at an open, mountainside terrace that Mordred created out of the black sludge with a snap of his fingers. They sat down at a table beneath the star-filled sky and Mordred handed her a large black box.

"For you," he said, "and what you're about to do for me."

Psy-chick opened the box and saw the biggest, brightest diamond in all of known history lying inside. She sighed and closed the box shut.

"Thank you, Mordred," she said.

The Shadow Prince looked at her questioningly. "You don't like it? It doesn't impress you?"

"No," Psy-chick assured him. "It's wonderful. It's just that . . ."

"Please, Psy-chick," Mordred said, "whatever it is you can tell me."

Ha! Right! Psy-chick thought. On the heels of that thought came another. *What the hurl? Why not?*

Psy-chick pushed back from the table and crossed her arms.

"Well, it's just that's all I am to you, isn't it? Just another subject whose sole purpose is to do your bidding."

"And can there be any greater purpose? I am a prince after all. One might say the greatest of all princes."

Psy-chick's gaze narrowed.

"Titles mean nothing without the proper actions to support them. Those in power should be servants to those who serve them. Heck, that's how we should all behave. That's the greatest purpose of all."

Mordred tilted his head.

"I'm not sure I follow you."

"It's what I've been trying to tell you since I came here, Mordred. My teammates and I stick with each other because we want to. Not because someone forces us to."

"It's mutually beneficial for you to do so?"

"Well, yeah. But that's not why we do it. We'd hang tough even if we didn't get anything out of it.

"We have each other's backs because we care about one another more than we care about ourselves. In short, we stick together because we are friends."

"Ah, there it is. We're to it at last—friendship." Mordred leaned forward and looked Psy-chick directly in the eye. "So what you're saying is, friends are loyal to one another not because they must be so due to station or bloodlines, but simply because they wish to be?"

"Yes! Exactly! Friends are the family you find, not just the one you're born into."

Mordred leaned back in his chair.

"Hmmm. Interesting concept. I don't guess I've ever had any friends."

"Seriously?" Psy-chick asked.

"Well, Mykal and Gebryal hung out with me, but only because my father made them do so.

"Oh! Wait a minute! I had several pet ophanim. Do they count?"

"Did you feed them?"

"Well, no."

"Did you pet them? Take care of them?"

"No, I didn't."

"Then they don't count."

"Then I guess I haven't had any friends after all."

Mordred dropped his head and sat in silence. Psy-chick actually began to feel pity for him—at least, to a degree. It was Mordred's fault that Chance, Shocker, and SC were dead. And he still hadn't let her see her other teammates. Who knew what trouble they were really in?

Psy-chick had to get out of Shadow Tower, but she didn't have to stoop to Mordred's level in the meantime. She reached out and touched his hand and he looked up.

Psy-chick smiled at Mordred.

"Then allow me to be the first."

Mordred smiled back.

Ribbit came hopping and panting up the stairs leading from the mountain's interior out onto the terrace. He was dressed in a fancy waiter's jacket and carried a large dish covered with a silver dome.

"Ah, dinner," Mordred said at the sight of Ribbit.

"Sorry, master! *Ribbit*. Ribbit hear your call inside Shadow Tower! Ribbit get here as fast as Ribbit can! *Ribbit*."

"You should be sorry," Mordred said. "I summoned you minutes ago—"

Mordred caught Psy-chick giving him a cross look.

Mordred took in a deep breath of air. "What I mean to say, Ribbit, is that's perfectly all right."

Ribbit placed the dish on the table and removed the cover. An entire roasted animal sat on the tray, a piece of strange fruit in its mouth. Psy-chick steepled her hands and gazed at Mordred expectantly.

"Uh," the Shadow Prince said, "in fact, Ribbit, why don't you join us?"

Ribbit looked at Mordred as though he'd slapped him.

"Really? Ribbit eat with Shadow Prince and Pretty Girl?"

Mordred nodded his head, struggling visibly to do so.

"Sit down, Ribbit," Psy-chick said. "It's OK."

Ribbit sat and Psy-chick stood up and took a carving knife from the table in preparation to serve everyone. She was pleasantly shocked when Mordred stood and gestured for her to hand him the knife.

"Here," Mordred said, "let me do that. A prince should be a servant to those who serve him, after all."

"You honor us, my lord," Psy-chick said. "I am very impressed." And Psy-chick *was* impressed by the Shadow Prince. So much so she almost regretted that she was going to have to bring him down.

26

Despite the comfortable bed he lay on, Chance was
unable to sleep. He tried self-hypnosis exercises until the black
night sky faded into the drab gray that signaled daybreak
within the Shadow Zone.

This morning, despite the sky being its usual overcast hue,
Chance was actually able to see the sun rise over the buildings of Barter Town. Even at this earliest stage in the sun's
trek across the sky, Chance could see that two-thirds of it was
eclipsed by other celestial bodies.

And a little more of it disappears every day, Chance ob-
served.

Chance got to his feet, feeling relatively good despite his
lack of sleep. His self-induced hypnosis had dulled the pain of
the shadow-bite to an almost imperceptible level. The bubbling black ooze in the center of his palm had congealed into

a large, unmoving black scab. He was back in control of himself—at least for now.

Chance gathered his things and then woke the others so they could do the same. They got up, relieved themselves, then ate a bit of the food they had purchased the night before with the goods they won. Lastly, each took a much needed and appreciated bath.

Afterward, they left Barter Town and took up their journey through the twisted and tangled woodland.

What I wouldn't give for a hovercar! Chance thought.

Shocker must have been thinking along the same lines. "Can't the three of us hang on to you, pud, while you clear the forest in a few bounds?"

SC shrugged. "Chance and I tried that a couple of days ago. I almost squished him to death when we landed. I may have Iron Maiden's strength, but not the years she's had to master it."

Shocker shrugged in understanding.

They reached the edge of the forest that afternoon. Chance and the others took in the view beyond. The ruins of what once must have been a great, metropolitan city sprawled outward before them for miles.

"It could be Chicago, or New York," Shocker said.

"Yeah, after being devastated by a nuclear bomb!" Space Cadet added.

Looking at the city, Chance's hand began to hurt. "I don't like it."

Viz wrapped her arms around herself as if a chilling breeze

had just passed. "You're right to be wary. None of the gangs venture into the city. It's were the Creepers dwell."

"Creepers?" Chance asked.

"Spider-people, arachnians," Viz said. "Every gang calls them something different. They're not very fierce one-on-one. But when they attack in numbers—and that's how they always attack—nothing can stand against them!"

Chance's skin crawled. "Why did it have to be spiders? I hate spiders!"

"Yeah," Shocker said. "As if Shadowmen and leviathans weren't enough. Now we've added creepy web-walkers to the mix! This place just gets better and better!"

"I'll protect us, Shocker," SC said. "Don't worry."

"If we stay out of their way, they should stay out of ours," Viz said. "The Creepers won't risk open confrontation. They prefer to lure their prey into a situation where victory is assured, and then pounce. We should be okay so long as we don't do anything stupid."

"Can't we use the caves and go beneath?" Chance asked.

"I'm afraid not," Viz said. "The underground network doesn't begin again until we reach the city's other side. And to go around would add days to our journey."

Chance gritted his teeth. "Well, that's it, then. No use wasting any more time worrying about it. Let's go."

The four travelers headed down the mountainside. SC began to hum a familiar tune.

"*Hmmm-hmmm-hmmm, hmmm-hmmm-hmmm. Friendly neighborhood hmmm-hmmm-hmmm.*"

"Not funny, SC," Chance called over his shoulder.

"Sorry, Chance. Couldn't help myself."

The skeletons of the once-great skyscrapers loomed over the Outlaws like menacing giants. The silence was utter and deafening and it made Chance all the more ill at ease. He felt the weight of hundreds of eyes watching him from every broken-out window and shadowed doorway.

Chance looked up at a large billboard advertising the release of the latest album from an attractive young female pop singer he'd never heard of. Someone had painted BEWARE THE WHITE WIDOW across it in sloppy, oversized red letters.

I don't like the sound of that, he thought. *The sooner we get out of here, the better!*

They traveled through the entire city without speaking a word to one another, stopping only for nature's call, which they answered as a group, backs turned. It was understood that venturing off alone, even for a moment, here within the home of the Creepers, was suicide.

When they reached the final blocks leading out of the city, Chance allowed himself to relax a little. But his guard sprang up again when a soft cry came drifting down from the surrounding buildings.

"*Help me*," the voice called. It sounded as if it belonged to a frightened little girl.

The group froze in step, listening.

"*Help me.*"

"It's a trap," Viz whispered.

"Help me."

"I think it's coming from up there," SC said. He pointed to an especially tall building just across the street from them.

"Shocker?" Chance asked, his voice low.

Shocker shook his head. "I don't know, Chance. I feel there's something out there—a *lot* of somethings. But I'm not picking up any thoughts. From the Creepers or anyone else."

"That doesn't make any sense," SC said.

"It was the same thing with the sand-sharks. Maybe minds that have no connection to Earth—minds that are indigenous to the Shadow Zone—work differently from our own? I'm not sure. Psy-chick would probably know what to make of it, but I don't."

"Help me."

"I'm telling you it's a trap," Viz said, her tone urgent. "Going into that building is exactly what the Creepers want us to do!"

"Probably," Chance said. "But then again, there might be someone in there who needs our help. We can't be certain either way without checking it out."

"Well, I'm going in with you, then," Viz said.

"Help me."

"No you're not," Chance said.

"But—"

"I need you to stay out here in case we don't make it out." Chance took Viz by the shoulders. "You're the only one who knows the way. We can't afford to lose you."

Viz stared at the ground and shrugged.

"You up for this, SC?"

Space Cadet popped his knuckles. "You know it!"

"What about me, Hicksville?"

Chance placed his hand on his friend's shoulder. "Hang out here with Viz."

"But—"

"Viz will need backup. Especially if we don't make it out. Can I count on you?"

Shocker nodded reluctantly.

"Good."

Chance and SC turned and started to walk away when Shocker threw his arms around their necks.

"Flarn Psy-chick and her hurling emotional mojo!"

They returned his embrace and then Chance and SC crossed the street to enter the building.

Chance sighed. "Why did it have to be spiders?"

He unsheathed his billy clubs and stepped through the building's entrance to disappear into the shadows.

27

"It's almost dawn, boy," Psy-chick said. She lay
against the dragon's neck, scratching behind its webbed, ele-
phantine ears. "I better go."

The dragon whined.

"Oh, now," Psy-chick said. "I should be back tonight."

Psy-chick got up and began to walk out of the cavern. The
dragon scuttled around her to block off the exit and roar in
protest. The cavern shook with the noise.

"Tommie, no!" Psy-chick said, her tone cross. "Bad
dragon!"

Tommie hung his massive head and pouted as he lum-
bered out of Psy-chick's way.

"Oh, you big baby!" Psy-chick gave the dragon's muzzle a
final pat. "I'll see you later tonight."

Psy-chick emerged from the cave to see the nearly eclipsed
sun peeking over the horizon beyond Shadow Tower.

Mordred's home made the sun's sparse light appear insignificant by comparison.

"Always darkest before dawn," Psy-chick whispered and then stepped through the door.

She was instantly inside a hallway of Shadow Tower. No matter how many times she walked through one of the Tower's doorways, she never got used to the idea of crossing miles in microseconds.

Psy-chick left the corridor and headed up to her room for some much needed rest. As she rounded a corner for the staircase leading there, she looked up and saw Iron Maiden, Private Justice, and Gothika being marched down the hallway toward her by a group of Shadowmen.

Psy-chick inhaled in surprise and retreated back into the corridor. She threw her back against the wall just in time to avoid detection. She turned her head sideways to watch as her friends and the Shadowmen strode past.

What luck! Psy-chick thought. *Here I've been searching everywhere and the Shadowmen bring them right to me!*

She waited until they turned another corner up ahead and then took off after them.

Psy-chick followed them over the course of multiple floors and winding passageways. She made sure to mentally note each new direction they took. At last, fortune had begun to swing her way and she wasn't about to let it go to waste.

She watched from above as the guards and her friends descended into a cell block that looked like the interior of a shadow-colored beehive. Her friends approached three cells that stood side by side as though they had been through this routine many times before. They moved in silence with their heads down. They were definitely not acting like the happy-go-lucky cardplayers Mordred had shown her.

That todak! Psy-chick thought.

The Shadowmen waved their hands before the cell doors and they opened in a mass of retreating ichor. The Shadowmen guarding Private Justice shoved him inside. The Outlaw fell on his face.

"You leave him alone!" Iron Maiden screamed.

Gothika raised her arm. It stretched outward and cracked like a whip across the bullying Shadowman's face.

She has PJ's elasticity! Psy-chick thought. *They've all traded powers, like me!*

A blast from the Shadowmen guarding Gothika knocked her unconscious and then both she and Iron Maiden were tossed into their cells. The Shadowmen waved their hands over the open cells and the prison doors closed. All the Shadowmen but one turned and began to walk up the stairs to where Psy-chick sat watching.

"Time to make my exit."

Psy-chick beat her feet down the hallway and retreated to an adjoining floor.

Don't worry guys, I'll be back!

She turned a corner and almost ran face-first into Mordred. He caught her at the shoulders before they could collide.

"Psy-chick?" he asked. "What are you doing down here at this hour?"

Oh, no! Psy-chick thought. *I'm done! It's over!*

"I, uh," Psy-chick said, struggling to think of a believable story. But lying had never been her strong suit. Psy-chick winced as the truth began to fall out of her mouth. "I was, uh, feeding the dragon?"

Mordred cocked an eyebrow as he studied her. Then a smile crossed his face and he laughed.

"You three-dimensionals have the absolute best sense of humor!"

Psy-chick breathed an inward sigh of relief as she forced herself to laugh. "That's us three-Ds: always kidding!"

"Well, actually," Mordred said, "I'm very glad I ran into you."

"Oh?" Psy-chick asked.

"Yes! It seems your old friend, and my new one, Ribbit, has decided to put on a one-man show in our honor tonight."

"You don't say?" Psy-chick asked, genuinely surprised. "I didn't know Ribbit was such an entertainer."

"Nor did I. But you find out all kinds of cool things about people when you make friends with them. Right . . . *buddy?*"

Psy-chick feigned a smile. "Exactamundo, pal."

"Great," Mordred said. "I'm off to commune with the Tower. I'll see you tonight."

"Tonight then."

Mordred's Chance-husk dissimilated and sank into the floor. Psy-chick sagged where she stood as she wiped away the sweat that had beaded up on her forehead. She turned and entered a staircase leading to her bedroom and the brief respite from imprisonment that sleep would provide her.

That evening, Mordred appeared before Psy-chick dressed in a neo-Victorian suit.

"My, my," Psy-chick said, "don't you look handsome to-night."

Mordred gave her Chance's bashful, crooked grin and Psy-chick felt her cheeks warm.

"Only to be surpassed by you, Psy-chick."

Mordred twirled his fingers and Psy-chick's already ornate dress blossomed into a full, sparkling gown of silver and gold with a long, flowing train. An accompanying raven-inspired hat and a luxurious shawl appeared, completing her outfit.

"Mordred," Psy-chick said as she caressed the shawl, "it's beautiful!" This time, there was no falsehood to her words.

"So are you," Mordred said. "Shall we, friend?"

Psy-chick smiled and placed her gloved hand within that of the Shadow Prince.

That night, they ate outside by the soft, molten light given off from a set of naturally occurring lava falls in some far corner of the Shadow Zone. The conversation was pleasant and Psy-chick felt surprised, and a little guilty, to realize she was actually enjoying herself.

When it came time to attend Ribbit's performance, Mordred once again took her hand in his and they rode an ichor cocoon to a large stone amphitheater reminiscent of ancient Greece. In truth, that was not so far from the mark. Unbeknownst to Psy-chick, they were actually in the same ruins of Atlantis where Space Cadet had faced down the Minotaurs.

They took a seat along the front row and waited for Ribbit to make his debut.

When Ribbit came on stage dressed in a maestro's suit, Psy-chick began to clap and cheer. Mordred smiled and joined in.

"Good evening, lady and, *Ribbit*, gentleman! Ribbit now like to present to you, *Ribbit*, 'Pretty Girl and Shadow Prince: An Evening with Ribbit.' *Ribbit*."

Psy-chick and Mordred clapped again.

Ribbit cleared his throat, said his favorite word a few times, and then began to sing. The song was in some alien dialect and Psy-chick didn't understand the words, but it didn't matter. Unlike his usual speech, Ribbit's voice was a melodious tenor that never faltered. It was as though by singing, Ribbit was tapping into some beautiful, forgotten part of himself. Psy-chick sat watching in wide-eyed amazement.

When Ribbit finished, she gave him a standing ovation. She tugged on Mordred's arm until he followed suit. Ribbit bowed and left the stage to prepare for the next act.

"That was amazing!" Psy-chick said.

"Yes," Mordred agreed. "I'm disappointed this is the first time I've ever heard him sing. It was wonderful."

Mordred turned and faced Psy-chick. "Having friends is wonderful."

Psy-chick smiled at him and patted his hand.

Maybe there's another way? she thought. *Maybe I can talk him into letting us go? Maybe . . .*

Psy-chick's thoughts trailed off as Ribbit waddled back onto the stage, his hands behind his back. She and Mordred clapped again and Ribbit took a second bow.

Ribbit waited until they stopped and then began to speak in an error-free, singsong voice.

My name is Ribbit and sometimes I smell.
I have the face of a frog and I eat like a whale!

Psy-chick giggled. Mordred laughed and slapped his knee.

Ribbit brought one of his hands out from behind his back. It held a paper mask unmistakably made to look like Psy-chick. He put it in front of his face and began to talk again in a singsong voice, this time a high falsetto.

I am Pretty Girl with looks so fair.
I talk and talk and talk and talk but make sense only
    rare!

Psy-chick bent over and held her sides as she guffawed with laughter. Mordred wiped tears from his eyes as he tried to keep from doing the same.

Ribbit removed the mask and brought out the other he'd

been holding behind his back. It bore Chance's face but had red streamers an either side of the nose to depict Mordred's eyes. Ribbit put it up to his face and puffed out his chest.

I am the Shadow Prince, you better do what I ask!
Or I'll scream, holler, and kick like a big jack—!

Psy-chick gasped when Mordred appeared on stage and seized Ribbit by his throat. She glanced over to Mordred's empty seat to be sure this was actually happening.

"How dare you!" Mordred cried, his crimson eyes blazing.

"Please, Mordred," Psy-chick begged, "don't do this!" She stood. "Ribbit didn't mean anything."

Mordred snapped his head in Psy-chick's direction.

"Is this what friends do, Psy-chick? Mock you? Betray you? I could've stayed in my father's house if I'd wanted to endure such!"

"He was just having some fun. He just wanted us to laugh!"

"I AM THE SHADOW PRINCE!" Mordred boomed. Lightning split the sky and thunder shook the amphitheater. "NO ONE LAUGHS AT ME! NO ONE!"

Mordred hurled Ribbit out into the amphitheater. He went limp as he landed against the hard stone seats. Psy-chick rushed over to him.

Ribbit lay there, bawling as he cradled his left arm. Psy-chick checked him over.

"Your arm's broken, Ribbit," Psy-chick said. "But if we put it in a splint you'll be OK."

Psy-chick whirled to face Mordred.

"He just wanted to be your friend! You could have killed him!"

Psy-chick jerked back as Mordred zipped over to her so fast it looked as though he had vanished from the stage and reappeared directly in front of her.

"Friends are for the foolish and the weak!" Mordred spat. "I should never have listened to you."

Mordred snapped his fingers and Psy-chick found herself once again alone in her bedroom.

"To think I'd begun to feel sorry for him," Psy-chick said under her breath. "But if that's how the todak wants to play, that's fine with me! It makes things a lot less complicated."

Psy-chick went into the dining room and began to pack Tommie's dinner.

28

Chance and SC walked through the building's foyer into a long hallway lined with abandoned, vandalized shops.

"This must have been a mall," SC said.

"No, a hotel," Chance corrected. "I can see the front desk up ahead. These are just novelty shops leading up to the main lobby."

"Beware the White Widow," Space Cadet said.

Startled by Space Cadet's words, Chance whirled to face him, billy clubs held at the ready. Chance relaxed when he realized his teammate had been merely reading the familiar words. They were painted across a storefront from floor to ceiling.

"That was on a billboard outside, too," SC said.

"Yeah, I saw it. We better be careful."

"You can say that again."

They reached the darkened lobby, passed by the front

desk, and entered a courtyard that stretched upward for countless stories. The hotel's rooms and the balconies that extended from them lined the courtyard's walls. The room was sparsely illuminated by a broken-out skylight. It was the shafts of light streaming down from it that allowed them to see the gargantuan spiderweb filling the courtyard's uppermost parts.

"Ugh!" Space Cadet said as he grabbed his nose. "What is that? It smells like rotted meat!"

"That's exactly what it is, SC," Chance said as he gazed up at the multiple cocoons hanging on the web's lower parts.

"Help me."

Chance sheathed his billy clubs and took out a pair of mini-binoculars from his utility belt. He peered through them up at the spiderweb. A beautiful young girl with pale skin and hair so blond it was almost translucent was fastened to the web's center in a half-spun cocoon.

"She's up there," Chance said as he returned the binoculars to their case in his belt, "dead center of the web."

"Wonderful," SC said. "So what's the plan, Chance?"

"Simple," Chance said. "We go up there and bring her down without anyone getting hurt."

"What about the Creepers?"

"Them, you can hurt!"

"Will your grappling gun reach?"

"Not from here. And that web is too thick to get a clean shot through to the other side. Otherwise, I would swing over, grab her, and then swing on over."

"Guess it's the hard way, then."

"Yep. 'Fraid so."

They found a stairwell and climbed several stories until they reached the bottom of the web where it attached to the balconies.

"Don't worry," Chance called to the girl. "We're coming to get you!"

She smiled back at them, her eyes full of gratitude.

"Where angels fear to tread," Chance said. He climbed over the balcony rail onto the spiderweb. Chance sidestepped several yards down the length of a large strand, walking it like a tightrope.

"It's springy," Chance said, "like a bungee cord."

Space Cadet sighed, grabbed a strand of web, and then placed a foot on the strand where Chance walked to follow him out. It sagged beneath his abundant weight. Chance flailed his arms frantically in the air to maintain his balance. SC drew back his foot. Both Chance and the strand bounced up slightly and then steadied.

"I'll try it again," SC said.

"No, SC! Don't—"

SC put his foot out on the strand and it broke. He twisted his body around and snagged hold of the balcony to keep from falling. Chance was not so lucky.

He fell through the air, plunging through wisps of web, the broken webstrand trailing behind him. Instinct told him to scream and grasp wildly at handholds that weren't there. But training took over and saved him.

He turned and snagged the broken webstrand where it fell

through the air behind him. It stretched and stretched and then, at last, recoiled hard, slinging him back up into the web.

As he landed, Chance wrapped his arms around two thick webstrands. His transferred motion made them quiver, but they held.

Chance exhaled in relief. Thank heaven!

"Are you all right?" the girl called down to him.

"I'm sooo sorry, Chance!" Space Cadet said.

"I'm fine," Chance called to them both. "A little shaken up, but no harm done.

"SC, looks like you're going to have to sit this one out, after all."

"Sorry, Chance."

"Don't worry. Just keep your eyes peeled. Anything moves, holler!"

"Holler?"

"Yell, SC. Yell!"

"Oh. OK."

"Please hurry," the girl pleaded.

Chance readied himself and then began the long, arduous climb to the web's center. He flinched every time he took a new step or handhold as the strands shook with his every movement.

Why did it have to be spiders? Chance thought again as the lump in his throat tightened.

Chance pressed on, trying not to think about it. After some time, he reached the web's nexus and the girl.

"I'm Chance Fortune. I'm going to get you out of here."

"Oh, thank you!" the girl said as she fluttered her long, wispy eyelashes at him.

Chance smiled. The girl was small and frail, but that only added to her beauty. She had the kind of face you could look at for hours without ever realizing where the time went.

Chance shook his head and removed his cutting laser from his utility belt.

Should be dry by now, he thought.

"We'll have you out of here lickety-split!"

Chance cut her cocoon from the web and pulled her upright. Her eyes met his and he was once again momentarily lost.

"Uh, now to cut you out of this thing," Chance said as he aimed his laser-cutter at the cocoon.

"Chance!" SC screamed.

Chance jerked his head in SC's direction to see his teammate ripping the remains of a webbing-gag from his face. An eight-legged creature covered in dense black fur stood before him. It glared at SC with multiple pairs of eyes as it hissed.

Space Cadet bared his teeth and swatted the creature off the balcony with the back of his hand.

"Creepers!"

Chance looked up to see that they were surrounded. Drooling, fanged Creepers covered their every route of escape.

"Are you certain we can't talk this over?" Chance asked, slowly easing down the laser-cutter's intensity with his thumb. The Creepers might be killers, but he wasn't. Captain Fearless had taught him better than that.

The Creepers hissed in reply.

"I thought not."

One of the creatures charged toward them. Chance shined the cutter in its eyes. The Creeper halted in its tracks and raised its forelegs to its face. Chance dropped the cutter to grab an above-hanging webstrand with his free hand.

He used it to balance himself as he kicked the Creeper with both feet. The creature went tumbling down through the webbing, knocking others out of the way as it fell.

Chance hugged the girl to him and swan-dived through the opening left in the Creeper's wake. She screamed as they fell. Chance ignored her, not having time to comfort and console.

Chance felt something snag his back and he and the girl ceased falling only to spring up in the opposite direction. He reached behind him and ripped a thick, silken strand from his back just as the Creepers renewed their attack.

Chance kicked and punched, transferring the cocooned screaming girl from hand to hand and hand to boot so that he could fend off his attackers from all directions, just keeping his balance all the while. It was a ballet of fisticuffs and equilibrium rivaling any circus high-wire act.

Chance looked down to see SC readying to sling a chair. They traded thumbs-up and then Chance returned to his midair struggle.

As Chance was moving the girl to the bridge of his foot so that he could let loose with a massive uppercut, the icy fire of the shadow-bite shot up his arm and into his torso.

"Ah!" Chance screamed. "Not now!"

The girl began to drop. Chance reacted, ignoring his pain.

In a fraction of a second, Chance grabbed hold of the web with one arm, swung his upper body down to trade places with his lower body, simultaneously kicking his attacker away and snatching the girl with his wounded hand before she could fall. But the reprieve was short-lived.

The girl let loose with a new torrent of screams as the cocoon threads Chance held her by began to pop and give way. She dropped several inches as Chance struggled on, now having to rely solely on his feet to keep the Creepers at bay.

The threads gave some more and the girl shrieked as she dropped to dangle a full foot beneath Chance's hand.

"SC!" Chance yelled as he kicked and held with everything he had. "Her cocoon's not going to hold! She's going to fall, SC!"

Space Cadet knocked the heads of two Creepers together. They dropped unconscious onto a knee-deep pile of others along the balcony.

"What do you want me to do, Chance?"

"You've got to jump and catch her when she does!"

"I can't, Chance. We tried that, remember? I almost killed you!"

Chance put his boot-heel into the back of a Creeper and the threads of the girl's cocoon made a sound like a shirt being torn in two. Her screams sounded anew as she dropped another foot.

"Yes, you can! You can do this, SC! You can!"

There was an eternity-long moment of silence. "OK, Chance. I'll try—no, I'll do it!"

"Thatta boy! I knew—" The most agonizing bolt of pain yet ran up Chance's arm and he let go of the girl, unable to help himself.

SC's eyes grew wide as he watched the girl fall. Then they narrowed and he yelled as he kicked off from the balcony with all his might.

Space Cadet flew through the air, the wind whistling across his face, his trajectory taking him directly into the screaming girl's path.

He reached the girl and bobbled her in his hands for several heart-stopping seconds before finally enveloping her in his arms. They began to drop and SC swung himself around so that it was his back that absorbed the impact as they crashed through several balconies and finally hit the ground.

"Run!" Chance screamed to them as he continued fighting off Creepers.

SC hopped up, slung the still semi-bound and still screaming girl across his shoulder, and bolted for the hotel lobby.

Chance knocked away the Creepers within his immediate vicinity and then took off his utility belt. He slapped it over an outward-bound strand and kicked off, riding it like a zip-line to an adjoining balcony.

He let go of his belt with one hand and dropped onto the balcony directly below. He rolled to his feet and refastened his utility belt around his waist. Then he sprinted for the stairwell as fast as his legs would take him.

A few battered Creepers later, he was outside with the group once again. He walked over and put his hands on his knees, exhausted beyond belief.

"I was just about to go in and save you!" Shocker said as he slapped Chance on the shoulder.

"Gee, thanks," Chance said. "Now let's get the hurl out of here before those Creepers decide to come after us!"

The group broke into a jog. The rescued girl seemed content to let Space Cadet carry her in his arms, and he was overjoyed to do it. In no time they were out of the city and far away from the Creepers, but the true danger was only just beginning.

29

"Idiots," Viz said as she slapped a small bug from her shoulder. "I should've known better than to throw my lot in with Brotherhood wannabes!"

Even though the mostly eclipsed sun had set and rose again since their confrontation in what everyone had come to think of as Creeper City, she was still fuming over Chance's decision to enter the building.

She and the others now sat on dead logs scattered in a dense marshland taking a much needed break from their journey—although it was hard to rest with bugs swarming all around them.

"Don't let her fool you," Shocker whispered to Chance. "For all her talk, she wanted to go in and save you in Creeper City. She was worried about you, Hicksville!"

Chance cut his eyes in Shocker's direction.

"No way."

Shocker's eyebrows raised above his sunglasses.

"I mean *really* worried."

Chance looked to Viz and then back at Shocker, his cheeks reddening.

"But I made her stay," Shocker continued. "Like you said, I'd never find Iron Maiden and the others without her, and I knew that's what you'd want."

"You did right, Shocker," Chance said. "You did right."

"Who's the girl?" Shocker asked, still whispering. "She still hasn't told the rest of us her name."

"I don't know her name either," Chance said. "But there hasn't exactly been time for small talk up until now. Anyway, isn't she gorgeous?"

"She's that, all right," Shocker said. "Though that still doesn't answer my question."

"Well," Chance said, "why don't you tell me who she is? You're the psychic, after all."

"That's what bothers me, Chance. Like everything else in the Shadow Zone not connected in some way to Earth, I get nothing from her. And look at the bugs. We're swarmed, but there's not a single one around her!"

"So, she's a native? So what? Look at her. Does she look dangerous to you?"

They both turned and watched as the girl giggled and played patty-cake with SC. Chance grinned from ear to ear, unable to take his eyes off of her.

"She sure is a silly little thing," Shocker said.

"What do you mean by that?" Chance asked, his face hardening.

"I mean look at her," Shocker said. He imitated the girl's overly feminine, overly childish mannerisms. "Patty-cake, patty-cake, baker man!

"You got to be kidding me, right? I mean, I haven't seen such a bimbo act since Missy Miracle's sugary-sweet kiss-up routine in Professor Xenoman's class!"

Chance spun to face Shocker. "You take that back!"

Viz stood up, placing her hand on her bo staff. SC and the girl stopped their playing and went silent.

"OK, OK," Shocker said. "Take it easy, Hicksville!"

"You're always running your mouth," Chance said. His right hand curled into a fist. "Someday someone's going to come along and shut it for you!"

"This isn't you, Chance," Shocker said. "What's gotten into you?"

"Oh, it's me all right! The *me* I should've been with you a long time ago!"

Chance felt a surge of force within his right hand just before it shot out and grabbed Shocker by the front of his shirt. Chance brought up his left to strike only for Viz to entangle it within her bo staff.

Chance felt a vice seize his right wrist and looked to see Space Cadet holding his arm.

"Let Shocker go, Chance," SC said, an uncharacteristic sternness in his voice.

Chance's forearm thrummed with icy fire beneath SC's grip. For a moment, Chance was sure he could break free. He could knock SC away and then make him and the other two pay for daring to defy him.

Then Captain Fearless's voice spoke inside his head—*What are you doing, lad?*—and whatever feelings had seized him shrank away and then left all together.

Chance's body sagged with great fatigue. He let go of Shocker and SC and Viz let go of him in turn. Chance glanced at his right hand, peering at it as if it were some alien creature.

Isn't it? Chance thought.

"I—" Chance said, fumbling for words, "I'm sorry, Shocker. I don't know what came over me."

"It's all right, Chance," Shocker said as he straightened his shirt. "We've all had a long few days. It's got us on edge. We just need to get some rest. That's all."

"I'm . . ." Chance said, his words still coming slowly, "I'm going to . . . go clear my head. I'll be back in a bit."

"Don't be long," Viz warned. "The sun is already setting. Or at least what's left of it."

Chance wandered off alone into the marsh and entered another clearing. He did mental relaxation exercises as he slowed his breathing. After some time, he was able to calm down and ease the ache within his arm.

You're losing it, Josh! Chance thought. He, of course, still thought of himself as Josh Blevins, the small-town boy from Tennessee. Chance Fortune was the guy his teammates looked up to—the superhuman who never made mistakes or let anyone down. Chance Fortune always knew what to do and he most certainly never snapped at his friends or lost it in a crisis situation.

And right now, Chance thought, *you're about as far away from Chance Fortune as you can get!*

Chance's hand began to hurt again. He couldn't help but think that his self-doubt and negativity had everything to do with that.

He turned and stared at a tall flower that stood in the clearing's center. He began his relaxation exercises again, gazing at the flower's brilliant, rainbow-colored petals.

"So beautiful," he mumbled as he gazed at the flower. "Like the girl, so beau—"

Suddenly, Chance was no longer in the marshlands outside Creeper City. Heck, he wasn't even in the Shadow Zone!

Chance heard hundreds of people screaming his name—*his real name.*

"Josh! Josh! Josh!"

He looked up and saw he was in a football stadium—the home field of a high school team by the look of it—overflowing with orange-and-black-clad fans chanting his name.

Utterly confused, he realized his view of the scene was divided into a grid by the facemask of a football helmet—one that he was wearing.

Chance heard someone growling and turned his head to see a large purple-and-white-clad football player sprinting toward him.

Chance waited until the last second and then sidestepped him. The football player dived and missed Chance, and slid along the grass on his belly. Chance read the word *INVIN-CIBLES* above the numbers on the player's jersey.

What the hurl is going on here? Chance thought.

"What are you doing, Josh?"

Chance turned to see Shocker beside him. Shocker, no, that wasn't right. This boy's name was *Shockley*—and he was dressed in a black and orange football uniform.

"Run!" Shockley screamed.

"What?" Chance asked. His entire world had been turned upside-down in a matter of seconds.

"Run," Shockley repeated, "I'll block for you. Now run!"

Chance looked down and saw that he held a football in his right hand. When he looked up, Shockley was sprinting down the field ahead of him. Without further thought, he tucked the football in the crook of his arm and took off after him for the end zone on the field's other side.

30

The Outlaws, all forty of them, hoisted Chance above their padded, orange and black clad shoulders, parading him up and down the field after his game-winning touchdown run. Chance held his helmet aloft, yelling shouts of victory.

It wasn't long before the Outlaws' fans came pouring out of the stands to mob them. Many even climbed and toppled the goalpost in the end zone where Chance had scored to win the big game.

Chance heard a familiar voice calling, "Josh! Josh!" and looked to see SC—no, not SC, *Percy*—fighting his way through the crowd toward him. Percy wore an orange-and-black band uniform and had a large tuba encircling his equally large waist.

Chance reached down and high-fived his friend before being swept back up into the air. When they put him down again, he stood among several orange-and-black-clad teenage cheerleaders pushing and shoving one another in order to be the first in line to give him a congratulatory hug.

A pretty girl dressed in jeans and a letterman's jacket—Chance's letterman jacket—elbowed her way to the front and enveloped him within her arms.

"Psy-chick!" Chance said, his eyes wide with surprise.

She pressed her mouth to his and Chance forgot about the strangeness of his situation. In fact, he forgot about everything.

"Who's Psy-chick?" the girl asked when at last she drew back. "I know you're running on an adrenaline high right now, but don't you even know your own girlfriend?"

"Of course I do . . . ?"

"Helena!" the girl said as she playfully slapped his chest. "Now quit teasing me, you big goof! A game-winning goof, but still a goof!"

"Josh!"

Chance turned and saw his mother charging through the crowd toward him, his younger brother Jacob at her heels. She wrapped him in a bear hug and covered his face with quick, machine-gun kisses.

Chance felt a large, strong hand grip his shoulder.

"I'm so proud of you, son."

Chance looked up and his breath caught in his throat.

"Dad?"

Chance looked into the face of his father, John Blevins. John's brown hair was gray at the temples and there were far more wrinkles around his eyes than when Chance had last seen him. That had been just before his father's suicide.

But there could be no doubt, it was John. It was his father, alive and well after all these years.

Chance threw himself against his father, wrapping his arms around his waist and pressing his cheek against his shirted chest. Tears swelled in Chance's eyes.

"Are you OK, son?" John asked.

"Never better, Dad!" Chance said. "Never better!"

His father's arm across his shoulders, Chance and his family and friends began to walk down the green toward the field house containing the Outlaws' locker room.

"Chance!" an old man's voice called. "Chance! Over here, lad! It's me! Captain Fearless!"

Chance turned and saw a silver-haired man sitting in the stands waving a long black cane at him.

"Who's that, Josh?" John asked. "And why is he calling you 'Chance'?"

Chance studied the old man for several minutes. Do I know him? Chance couldn't recall. There was something at the back of his mind—not so much a memory as a gnawing sensation—trying to push its way to the surface, but falling just short.

All is not right, here, Chance thought. *There's something about that old man. Something*—but then it was gone.

Chance shrugged. "I don't know, Dad. I probably remind him of someone he knew. Or maybe he's just old and delusional. This 'Chance' probably never existed at all."

Chance stood gazing at the old man while John and the rest of the group walked on ahead.

"You coming, son?" John asked. "You know Harvey serves

free cheeseburgers to the team after a win. You're going to miss out!"

A passing spectator stepped in Chance's line of sight. When he stepped out, Captain Fearless and Chance's memory of him and everything else that had occurred within the past five years was gone.

"Coming, Dad," Chance—*Josh*—said.

Shocker looked up at the Shadow Zone's two moons, a worried expression on his face. Chance had been gone now for several hours.

"Flarn it, Hicksville, where are you?" Shocker asked. "We could be up to our armpits in Shadowmen at any moment!"

"I'm going to go look for him," Viz said. She picked up her bo staff and stood.

"I'm going with you," Shocker said. He pointed his thumb at SC and the girl. "Anywhere they can hide?"

"There's an entrance to the next set of caves about a hundred yards north of here," Viz said.

"Good," Shocker said. "If we're not back in half an hour, head that way, SC—Space Cadet?"

Space Cadet and the girl sat on a log whispering in each other's ear as they giggled with abandon. It had been a non-stop flirt-fest between them since she'd joined the group. The infatuation for the girl Shocker felt radiating from SC was so strong that it made him want to vomit.

"Yo! SC!" Shocker said after he didn't get their attention the first time.

SC whipped his head around in surprise. "Uh, yeah?"

"Did you hear me?" Shocker asked.

"Sure," SC said, already turning his attention back to the girl, "the caves. Half an hour."

Shocker shook his head and then followed Viz out of the clearing.

They walked in silence for several moments, then Shocker spoke.

"So what is it you know about Chance that you're not telling us?"

"I don't know what you're talking about."

"Oh, come on. Don't play coy with me. I can push through and read that mind of yours, if I have to."

"Mind your manners with me, Brotherhood stooge, or I'll mind them for you!"

"Okay. Okay. Let's not get off track, here. I didn't mean to upset you. I'm just worried about my friend. And I can't help him if you won't tell me what's wrong. So, please, tell me. I'm on my knees here, begging."

"He told me not to tell."

"Ah-ha! I knew it! It would be just like Hicksville not to want us to worry about him. But with the dire situation of our friends being held captive, whatever it is, it must be bad if he asked you to keep it a secret from us."

"The worst."

"We're to it, now," Shocker said. "You might as well go on and tell me."

"Chance has been infected by a Shadowman," Viz choked out. "When he saved me on the cliffs, he was bitten on the hand. The poison has been slowly spreading through his body and it's finally begun to take its toll on him. It's amazing he's held out this long!"

"What's going to happen to him?" Shocker asked.

"If he's as lucky as you say," Viz said, "*death*."

Shocker paused in step for a moment, and then continued on. "And if he's not so lucky?"

"Well," Viz began. But her words were cut short by an ear-piercing scream.

"That's SC!" Shocker yelled. He turned and ran back down the path, Viz at his heels.

31

"Bottom!"

Josh watched as his shot from the three-point line marked on the carport in his backyard flew through the air in a perfect semicircular arc to drop cleanly through the basketball hoop mounted on their home's garage.

"That's it!" Helena said as she threw up her hands in defeat. "I can't take any more humiliation. I'm going home."

"Ah come on!" Josh protested. "One more game."

"Nope! That's it for me."

"Oooky," Josh said as he approached her. "I promise to take it easy on you next time."

"Whatever!" Helena said. She smiled and rolled her eyes. They shared a quick, parting kiss.

"See you later, alligator," Chance said.

Helena, already walking away, turned around and said "After awhile, Gomer Pyle!"

"Ha," Josh said. "Good one!"

"Learned from the best."

Josh watched her walk the first of the three blocks between their houses and then turned to see his dad standing beneath the hoop holding the basketball.

"Care for a little one-on-one with the Old Man?" Mr. Blevins asked.

"It's your funeral," Josh said.

"Ha! We'll see." John walked to the end of the carport. "Check," he bounced the ball to Josh.

Josh bounced it back to his father as he stepped onto the court. "Check."

Mr. Blevins advanced, his back between Josh and the ball. He faked with his head left, then right. Josh took the bate on the second one and his father rolled around him to lay it up for a basket.

"Two—nothing!" Mr. Blevins said.

"Yeah, whatever."

Josh took the ball to the end of the carport and bounced it to his father. "Check."

Mr. Blevins bounced it back as Josh stepped onto the carport. "Check."

"Dad," Josh said as he stood there dribbling.

"Yeah, son?"

"Has anything seemed weird to you this past week?"

"What do you mean?"

"I don't know. Just little things."

"Like what?"

"I was out here all afternoon with Helena. I didn't miss a single shot!"

"Your Papaw always said it was better to be lucky than good!"

Josh charged forward like an oncoming train. Mr. Blevins scrambled backward, trying to keep his body between Josh and the goal. But Josh was quicker. He blew by his father and laid it up for two points.

"Too slow, old man," Josh said.

"Just giving you a false sense of security."

"Yeah, right!"

They returned to the end of the court and exchanged the ball.

"But not missing a single shot? That's better than lucky! That just doesn't happen."

"Oh, yeah?" Mr. Blevins advanced in a circular trajectory toward the three-point line.

"And that's not the only thing. I had five tests this week at school. I aced them all, one hundred percent!"

"You get your brains from your mother. She's as smart as a whip, and you're a chip off the old block."

"Dad, I didn't even study! It's like everything goes my way. Always!"

"Dreams are like that, but not real life."

Mr. Blevins let loose his shot. It went wide, banging off the backboard. Josh recovered it and took it back out to the court's end to continue play.

"And there's something . . . *weird*," Josh said.

"I remember when I was your age and started getting hair in funny places, son."

Josh charged ahead and put the ball up for another two.

"Dad, please! I'm not joking. This is something . . . *creepy*."

"Creepy?"

"Yeah, it's probably just my imagination playing tricks on me, but it's *weird*."

"Weird?"

They exchanged the ball at the court's end.

"Yeah," Josh continued. "Lately, no matter where I am, I've seen movement out of the corner of my eye. Quick movement, you know? Like someone sneaking up on me and then jerking back and holding still when I turn, hoping they won't get caught.

"But when I look, all I see is my shadow."

Mr. Blevins charged forward and knocked Josh off balance.

"Hey!" Josh cried. "Foul!"

"I didn't hear the ref blow his whistle."

Josh smirked at his father.

Mr. Blevins smiled back as he tossed Josh the ball. "Go ahead."

Josh went up to the painted foul line, the sun at his back.

He looked down as he dribbled the ball a couple of times, seeing his shadow-double do the same. Josh held the ball in his hands but kept looking at his shadow, waiting for something to happen. Then it did.

Josh scrambled backward in fright. "There!" he said as he pointed at his shadow. "Did you see that?"

"See what, son?"

"My shadow! It had eyes! They flashed red! Just for a second, but I swear they flashed red!"

"Josh," Mr. Blevins said, his voice full of concern. "Are you feeling all right?"

"You believe me, Dad. Don't you?"

Mr. Blevins paused in consideration. "I believe that between football and school you've been under a lot of stress lately. And when the body and mind are stressed too long, even normal things can seem strange."

"You think I'm crazy," Josh said and dropped his head.

Josh felt his father's hands grip his shoulders.

"Hey!"

Josh raised his head to peer up at his father.

"You're a Blevins," Mr. Blevins said. "Even better, you're my son. It's impossible that you're crazy. Maybe a little overwhelmed at the moment, but not crazy. No way. Not my boy!"

Josh's heart swelled with affection for his father. *I want to be just like you some day,* Josh thought. *I want to have my children look up to me the same way I do to you!*

Josh smiled. "Thanks, Dad. I love you."

"I love you, too, son."

"Dinner," Josh's mom cried from the house. Her head disappeared back inside just as quick as it had appeared.

Mr. Blevins hung his arm on Josh's shoulder as they turned and walked toward the house, ball in arm.

I was silly to ever question all this, Josh thought. A loving family. A great girlfriend. Excellence in academics and sports. Face it, Tiger, you've hit the jackpot!

But then he caught a glimpse of his shadow trailing along behind him. An eye that shouldn't have been in its head winked and Josh shivered.

32

"You are so funny!" the girl giggled.

"Oh, stop, it!" Space Cadet said as he feigned bashfulness, "I bet you say that to all the boys!"

The girl put her hands on his upper arm and kneaded it as though it were dough. "And so strong!"

"Now you're embarrassing me!" Space Cadet said. He smiled as he flexed his bicep for her.

"And so big!"

The girl reached down to pat SC's ample belly. That caught Space Cadet totally off-guard. But he enjoyed the girl's touch, so he let it be.

"Woo!" SC said. "Usually, we just shake hands around here!"

His words set them both giggling uncontrollably again. After a time, the girl caught her breath and wiped tears of laughter from her eyes.

"You know, SC, I always hoped some gallant hero would come rescue me. But I never dreamed it would be anyone as handsome and charming as you!"

To SC's pleasant surprise, the girl leaned forward and kissed him square on the mouth.

"I-I-I," SC stuttered, "I don't even know your—"

The girl placed her finger on Space Cadet's mouth, shushing him. Then she removed her hand and leaned forward again, puckering her lips. Space Cadet closed his eyes and did the same.

SC was shocked to feel something strike his face with such force that it knocked him backward. He opened his eyes to peer at the girl through a translucent cloud of silk.

"What are you—" SC began.

The girl opened her mouth. SC noticed that her canines had lengthened to a considerable degree. A silky, white substance shot out of the girl's mouth to strike Space Cadet in the chest. It knocked him back to lie flat against the log.

"What the hurl?" Space Cadet shouted. More of the white stuff shot out of the girl's mouth to cover SC's body. He tried to sit up but found he could not move, though he struggled with every ounce of Iron Maiden's strength. He was secured to the log—just like the girl herself had been secured to the Creeper's web.

Oh no! Space Cadet thought. *That's exactly what this white stuff is, webbing! But that can only mean—!*

SC watched in horror as the girl's lips curled back and her jaw unhinged to reveal several receding rows of fangs. Her slender fingers elongated into crooked, razor-sharp claws.

The last wisps of the cocoon fibers she'd been wearing as a dress fell away as her young girl's body swelled and transformed into a giant, segmented spider's abdomen. Both it and the eight arachnid legs that now protruded from it where void of hue. The only spot of color on its entire hideous body was a large, red hourglass shape emblazed on its stomach.

Beware the White Widow! SC thought.

The White Widow surged forward and SC screamed.

Shocker sprinted into the clearing. To his credit, he did not pause or run shrieking in horror when he saw the giant, white spider straddled over a SC-shaped cocoon.

He immediately recalled the billboard in the city of Creepers. *Beware the White Widow!*

He scooped up a tree branch from the swampland floor and hurled it at the beast. It struck home and the White Widow turned to face him, it's long, jittery legs maneuvering its truck-sized bulk with unbelievable speed and grace.

Shocker saw the thing had the girl's face, or at least what remained of it, and realized what had occurred. The brow of its now massive forehead furrowed and it hissed at the sight of him.

Well, what now, genius? Shocker thought.

The White Widow charged forward. Shocker stood frozen to the ground with fear. He felt someone vault off his shoulder and looked up to see Viz jumping through the air, her bo staff raised high above her head and ready to strike.

The Widow turned its attention to this new threat. It

ejected globs of webbing from its mouth. Viz knocked the first two away with her staff but the third hit her in the leg and sent her tumbling to the ground. She landed and her bo staff went skittering off in the opposite direction, toward Shocker.

The White Widow sprayed Viz where she lay with web from its mouth. Viz struggled for only a moment before being encased in a cocoon.

The Widow's jaw unhinged as it leaned down over Viz to have its dinner. That got Shocker moving. He scooped up Viz's staff and bolted underneath the monstrous arachnid to jab its belly.

Enraged, the White Widow forgot about Viz and scrambled around trying to rid itself of the nuisance. Shocker kept pace and managed to stay directly beneath the spider as he jabbed and gouged it with Viz's staff.

But Shocker was not prepared when the Widow suddenly flexed its gigantic legs and sprang straight up into the air.

The White Widow turned its massive bulk so that it came down directly behind Shocker.

Shocker dropped the staff and bolted from the clearing. The giant spider knocked trees and deadfall out of its way as it scurried after him. Shocker wanted to scream, but there was no time!

He spotted a large, hollow log ahead of him and dove inside just as the Widow lunged for him. It crashed against the log's opening, sending dust and debris flying as the rotten wood crumbled around it.

Shocker scrambled backward on his elbows as the monster

charged forward, splintering more and more of the rotten log into hundreds of pieces with each new lunge.

Shocker reached the log's end and clumsily got to his feet just as the Widow burst through the last bit of the deadfall. Now Shocker did scream!

He ran as fast as his legs would take him through several large hedges to stumble into a clearing.

Shocker looked up and what he saw halted him in his tracks. Chance stood motionless before him, his shoulders slumped. A large wildflower stood between the two of them in the clearing's center. Its rainbow-colored petals were wrapped around his captain's head.

"Chance?" Shocker asked in disbelief.

Shocker felt something pelt him in the back with the force of a Mack-truck. He tumbled to the ground, gasping for air. When at last his rolling stopped, Shocker looked up and saw the drooling, hissing face of the White Widow above him.

33

Josh sat curled up in bed, a single bedside lamp illuminating the drawing pad lying across his blanketed knees, when he heard a knock at his bedroom door.

"Enter!" he called.

The door opened to reveal Josh's father standing in the hallway. "Is that how you talk to your father, Josh? Or anyone else, for that matter?"

"Sorry, Dad."

Mr. Blevins walked over and sat on the edge of the bed beside Josh. He held out his hand. "Whatcha drawing, champ?"

Josh handed his father his drawing pad.

"Superheroes, again?" Mr. Blevins reprimanded. "I thought you'd outgrown this kind of stuff."

Josh shrugged. "They're just metaphors for humanity's potential. And besides, they're cool!"

Mr. Blevins shook his head and placed the drawing pad facedown on Josh's nightstand.

"Son, I've been thinking about our conversation from earlier today."

"Oh, yeah?"

"Yeah. And I think you're right. Things have been a little crazy around here lately. For all of us."

"I knew it!" Josh said. "I knew I couldn't be the only one!"

"That's why . . ."—a smile spread over Mr. Blevins's face as he reached into his back pocket—"I bought these!"

Mr. Blevins held out four airline tickets. Josh took them from his hand.

"These are to Hawaii," Josh said, confused.

"Yep!" Mr. Blevins said. "I think it's high time the Blevins family took a vacation. Don't you?"

"Uh, sure," Josh said, crestfallen.

"We'll pack in the morning and catch the afternoon flight. But don't tell your mom or your brother! I'm waiting to spring the news when they wake up tomorrow. Won't that be great?"

"Perfect, Dad. Just perfect. *Everything's perfect.*"

"Great! Then it's settled!"

Mr. Blevins playfully ruffled Josh's hair and then got up and walked to the door.

"I love you, big guy!" Mr. Blevins said, still grinning ear to ear.

"Love you, too, Dad."

Mr. Blevins turned and left the room, shutting the door

behind him. Josh sighed, turned off the lamp, and then sank down into his bed, pulling the covers up to his chest.

With the moonlight shining in from the window, Josh could still see much of his room. His eyes fixed on the louvered closet doors directly across from the foot of his bed. His breath caught in his throat when a pair of glowing red eyes appeared in the darkness on the doors' other side to stare back at him through the slats.

Josh thought about closing his eyes to see if whatever was in his closet would be gone when he reopened them, but decided against it. As scared as Josh was, he was tired of running from whatever phantom was haunting him.

"You're real, aren't you?" Josh asked. His voice was steady, but the sound of it cutting through the quiet dark creeped him out.

"Yes." The word was more growled than spoken.

"I'm not afraid of you," Josh said.

"But you are afraid, aren't you?"

Josh nodded. "I know you're real, but I'm afraid that nothing else is. I'm afraid, because as great as this life is, something tells me it's not really mine."

Tears began to leak from Josh's eyes.

"And I'm afraid that my dad, who I love more than anything, isn't really supposed to be here. I'm scared that by even speaking these words, I'm going to make him go away!"

Heavy, rhythmic breathing sounded from the closet. Josh thought it was the noise a dragon sleeping in its cave would make. Then the shadowy red-eyed thing spoke.

"You are not this Joshua Blevins. Not really. You are

Chance Fortune, a superhero in training, though you don't have any powers to speak of. At least, *not yet*.

"Right now, your face—your real face—is attached to a life-force eating flower in an alien swampland. It has created this false reality in your mind, keeping you in a comalike state so that you cannot resist its feeding upon you.

Josh drew the covers up to his chin.

"Meanwhile," the shadowed thing continued, "across the marsh, your friends—your real friends, not these perfect-world facsimiles—are under attack and will most certainly die unless you wake up and intervene."

Josh threw back his covers and sat up on the side of the bed.

"I know you!" Josh said. "You're the infection—the shadow-bite!"

Another long pause.

"Yes. But right now I'm your only hope at summoning the strength you need to break out of this dream and save your friends."

Josh startled as his drawing pad fell off his nightstand and landed on the floor faceup. Its pages flipped back of their own accord to show a remarkably lifelike sketching of an old man.

"Don't listen to it, lad!" the drawing said. "We can get you out of this together, you and I!"

"You—" Josh said, "you were in the stands the other day."

"I'm your mentor, lad. Captain Fearless. Or at least your mind's version!"

The drawing pad abruptly burst into flames.

"Senile old fool," the shadow-bite said. "Don't listen to him. It would be years before you got out of here doing anything his way, and your friends need help now! You wouldn't let them down, would you? Not when they need you the most?"

Josh stared at the smoldering pages of his drawing pad and then got out of bed. He took a step toward the closet.

"What do I need to do?"

"Let me out," the shadow-bite said. "All this time, you've been fighting me, and winning, incredibly!

"But I've learned my lesson. I don't want to take over. Not completely. Frankly, I think your will is just too strong for that. Not like the others."

Josh took another step toward the closet.

"I've learned from you," the shadow-bite said. "I've evolved. I don't have to answer to *him*, anymore."

Josh stepped back. "Him who?"

"Never mind," the shadowed thing insisted. "No one. It's not important. What *is* important is the fact that your friends are going to die if they don't get help right now!"

Josh gave the smoldering pages a last glance. Then he squared his jaw and charged for the closet doors. He threw them open as hard and as wide as he could.

34

Chance felt power and rage course up his arm and consume his entire body. The latter was not the normal fury of teenagers, the kind that burns white-hot and fades quickly. This rage was as cold and as black as death itself.

Chance's eyes popped open. The rainbow-colored flower's stigma hung before his face, glowing softly as it pulsed with the reception of the Outlaw's life force.

Then something within Chance's eyes flexed and the view before him changed. He was actually looking through the rainbow flower's petals. Before him, a giant spider-monster crouched over Shocker, ready to pounce.

Beware the White Widow, Chance thought.

Then another voice spoke up in his mind—that of the shadow-bite.

It's the Widow who need beware now. With my abilities and

your will, we are more powerful than any Creeper bride. We rival even the Shadow Prince himself!

"GET OFF HIM!" Laser beams shot from Chance's eyes through the flower to strike the Widow. The life-eating flower died immediately, engulfed in flames. The Widow shrieked in agony as the lasers continued their path to scorch her clear, chitinous shell.

Chance surged forward. The Widow spat globs of webbing at him as he advanced. Chance's eye-beams found each glob and sent them to the ground in flames.

Chance reached the Creeper queen and hit it so hard the surrounding trees bowed outward with the shock wave created by the force of the blow.

He gave the White Widow another earth-splitting right, then finished it off with an uppercut that sent it hurtling miles up into the air.

"Holy schnikees!" Shocker said as he joined Chance at his side. "You knocked it into orbit! How did you do that?"

"Things have changed, Shocker." Chance jerked the glove off his right hand. Black ichor coursed from his palm and crawled over his fist.

"Thanks to this, we are powerful now! Not puny like you. It was stupid of you to be out here at night by yourself."

"Well, that black soup sure hasn't done anything to improve your personality," Shocker mumbled.

Chance scowled as the whites of his eyes turned black with ichor. "What did you say?"

"Uh, nothing, Chance," Shocker said, his voice full of fear. "Nothing at all!"

"That's what we thought." The blackness in Chance's eyes receded. He put his glove back on and walked toward the clearing.

When he got there, he used his eye-beams to cut Viz and Space Cadet free from their cocoons.

"Wow!" Space Cadet said. His eyes were twin boiled eggs beneath his glasses. "Chance! You've got new super—"

"Can't we leave any of you alone to take care of yourselves for five minutes?" Chance interrupted. "You're all pathetic!"

"Uh," SC said. "Sorry, Chance?"

"Why are you acting this way?" Viz asked. "It's the shadow-bite, isn't it? It's given you these powers but made you hateful in the process."

"It's made us strong!" Chance corrected. "And about time, too. Now we can put the Shadow Prince in his place!"

"And save your friends," Viz said. "You do remember your friends, don't you?"

"Of course, we do," Chance said.

"It's long after dark," Shocker said. "We better head for the caves."

"The shadow-bite and I don't need the caves," Chance said. "Let the Shadowmen come. They'll only get what's coming to them."

"Well," Viz said, "I *do* need the caves. And I'm the only one who knows the way to Shadow Tower. I suggest you quit grandstanding and come along with the rest of us!"

Chance turned and looked at the horizon. "We don't need you to guide us to Shadow Tower anymore, Viz. We can see it!"

Chance began to lift into the air and Viz ran over and grabbed him by the arm.

"No, Chance," Viz pleaded. "Remember when you asked me what future I saw for you and your friends?"

"Yes," Chance barked. "What of it?"

"It was death, Chance! I saw death! If you go off half-cocked to Shadow Tower by yourself, someone is going to die!"

"You're absolutely right about that, Viz. The Shadow Prince's rule is over as of right now!"

The whites of Chance's eyes filled with ichor and then he launched into the air like a rocket, leaving his friends far behind.

35

Later that night, Psy-chick stood looking at her reflection in the parlor mirror. She gazed specifically at her night-princess-gown. It hung on her perfectly, hiding every flaw and emphasizing every attribute. Her eyes went to the sparkling diamonds at her neck and ears, and then on to the dark makeup around her eyes and lips.

The boons of tyranny and oppression, Psy-chick thought. How could I have ever thought this gown beautiful?

Psy-chick snarled as she tore the necklace from her throat. She flung it against the wall. It shattered and then decomposed into droplets of black ooze that melted into the floor. She tore off the earrings and wiped the makeup from her face, rubbing so hard it brought tears to her eyes. She violently ripped the gown from her body piece by piece until she stood in nothing but a pile of sinking ichor.

She left the parlor and went into her bedroom. She walked

over to her closet and opened the doors. Her old Burlington uniform hung inside, its starburst crest shining out at her from the black, leathery fabric.

"Time to take care of business!"

Psy-chick snatched the uniform from its hangar and slipped it on. Wearing it felt like being hugged by an old friend, one she'd thought almost lost to her.

Psy-chick strode into the dining area and grabbed the fully-packed satchel off the table.

"On second thought," Psy-chick said as she set the satchel back down, "I don't think Tommie will need this, after all."

Psy-chick went to the door leading from the parlor into the hallway and opened it, half-expecting to find Ribbit outside. But he was nowhere to be seen.

No telling where Mordred sent him, Psy-chick thought. *But if my plan works, it won't matter. He'll be as free as the rest of us.*

Psy-chick shut the door behind her, not bothering to look back. "Good riddance."

Psy-chick jogged down the hallway for the stairs, beginning the long trek to her friends' cell block. She retraced her steps, ducking for cover whenever she came across any patrolling Shadowmen. When at last she reached the platform above her friends' cells, she cursed to see two Shadowmen standing guard.

"Can't get a clear shot from here," she whispered. "I guess I'll have to try the direct approach."

She began to walk down the stairs leading to the cell block, praying that Mordred had gone out for the night and that the Shadowmen's mental communications with him were less than instantaneous.

"Hey guys," Psy-chick called as she exited the staircase.

The Shadowmen whirled in her direction, their eyes taking on a glowing red hue of warning.

"No, no, no," Psy-chick said. "You've got it all wrong. The Shadow Prince sent me."

The Shadowmen looked at each other in question, the red glow dissipating from their eyes.

"That's right," Psy-chick said as she approached, "he says I've been a very bad girl and that, for my own sake, you should lock me up."

Psy-chick walked up to the guards and held out her wrists as if she wanted to be handcuffed.

"Well, go ahead. What are you waiting for?"

The Shadowmen simultaneously reached out and grabbed Psy-chick's wrists. She immediately clasped theirs and sent hundreds of volts of electricity coursing through their bodies. The ichor drew away from their skin in patches as blue electricity crackled over it like hordes of sizzling serpents.

When Psy-chick let go, the smoking, inert bodies of the Shadowmen dropped to the ground and slumped against each other.

"If you can't take the heat . . ."

Psy-chick squatted down and took one of the Shadowmen's arms. The ichor was hot but solid beneath her fingers. She waved the arm in the direction of the three cells holding her friends. Each cell door came open as the Shadowman's hand passed over it.

"Come out guys, it's me, Psy-chick. I'm here to rescue you!"

Gothika was the first to poke her elongated neck outside her cell.

"Psy-chick? Is that really you?"

"In the flesh!"

Iron Maiden and Private Justice stepped out in turn. When they realized it was indeed their friend standing before them, they ran over and engulfed her in a multiple-bodied hug.

"Boy, are we glad to see you!" Private Justice said.

Psy-chick ruffled his flattop. "The feeling's mutual, PJ!"

"Where have you been?" Iron Maiden asked. "How did you escape?"

"That's a long story," Psy-chick said. "One I can tell you all later. Right now, we need to get out of here. For all I know, the Shadow Prince could show up at any moment."

"The Shadow who?"

"Trust me," Psy-chick said, "you don't want to know! But listen, if we don't stop him, his evil could spread throughout every known universe, including our own."

"What's the plan?" Iron Maiden asked.

"He's trying to escape from the Shadow Zone using a crude Infinity Chamber located at the top of this Tower. We've got to destroy it to ensure that can never happen."

"Roger that," PJ said. "Lead on!"

Psy-chick rocked backward as though she'd been dealt a blow.

"What's the matter?" Iron Maiden asked.

"It's just . . ." Psy-chick struggled for her words, "he said lead, and who would've thought? I mean, Chance should be—"

Gothika put her hand on Psy-chick's shoulder.

"Chance would be very proud of you right now."

"They all would be," Iron Maiden said.

Psy-chick nodded. "Then let's do this for them."

"For our friends," Private Justice said, "for our fallen brothers. Outlaws to the end!"

Without another word, Psy-chick headed for the staircase, her fellow Outlaws following closely. They advanced higher and higher through the tower until they could go no further. A final door stood before them, all passageways leading to it.

"This must be it," Psy-chick said.

"Can you open it using SC's technomancy, Maiden?" Gothika asked.

"No," Iron Maiden said, scratching her scarlet head, "it's like with our cell doors—this is not a straight technological structure. It has an arcane aspect to it. Perhaps if Private Justice used the magic he inherited from you and we worked together—"

"Stand back," Psy-chick said. "I've got this."

Psy-chick raised her arm and lightning leaped from it to obliterate the door in front of them.

When the smoke cleared, she breathed a sigh of relief to see the Vortex Chamber on the other side.

"OK," she said as they rushed inside. "Tear it up, from top to—"

Alarms began to blare all around them. A side door

opened and Dr. Faustoid bolted into the room. For a moment, he stared at the Outlaws in shocked amazement, and they at him. Private Justice recovered first and hurled a spell at the technomancer. Dr. Faustoid dodged and rolled to the ground.

"Chamber," Dr. Faustoid yelled, "activate defensive measures! Suppress and capture!"

A gun-turret dropped from the ceiling and sprayed Gothika with white foam. She stretched toward Dr. Faustoid, intending to bind him in her arms, but the foam formed a crystalline shell around her body before she made it halfway there. She was frozen solid.

Restraints sprung from the floor and snapped around Private Justice's ankles as a hologram of a three-dimensional pentagram encircled him. He tried to conjure his way out, but the spells only bounced back at him.

Another gun-turret dropped from the ceiling and fired a net that pinned Iron Maiden to the floor. Psy-chick saw a look of humiliation on her face. Once the demigoddess would have shredded through that netlike tissue paper.

"Psy-chick!" Iron Maiden's words were only partially discernible thanks to the net stretched over her mouth, "Look out!"

Psy-chick looked up and saw a transparent rubber dome dropping from the ceiling to ensnare her.

She tried to run, but it was too late. The dome slammed down, imprisoning her. She discharged electricity from her hands, but it was useless. They were trapped. She had failed and miserably so.

What would Chance think of you now, huh?

Mordred's ichor mass snaked down from the ceiling and took on its Chance-husk, adding insult to injury.

"What's going on here, Faustoid?"

"Master, I believe the key and her friends were attempting a coup d'état."

Mordred scowled and glided across the floor to stand face-to-face with Psy-chick.

"First the toad betrays me, now you."

Psy-chick hung her head.

"I shower you with luxury and wealth and you spit in my face."

Psy-chick snapped her head up. "And all it cost was their freedom and my soul."

Mordred's eyes flashed. "Very well, then. If these ants mean so much to you, you can spend the rest of your time until the eclipse alongside them in a cell."

Psy-chick blinked and found herself inside the same kind of cell that had held her friends. She was alone and surrounded by darkness. Psy-chick sank down against the cell wall, despair filling her heart. She wanted to pray for a miracle but decided her belief in them had died the same day as Chance.

36

Chance streaked through the night sky toward Shadow Tower, impervious to the wind's friction against his body. As he neared his objective, the vacuum created in his wake ripped many of the horse-head pumps from the ground and dragged them into the air to trail behind him.

Lightning crackled between the four pylons surrounding Shadow Tower, forming force-field walls between them. Chance flew ahead, undeterred. He struck a wall of the force field and passed through without slowing in speed. As he did so, the pylons exploded in a mass of fire and debris and the force field winked out of existence.

Chance looked ahead and saw black dots, which his new telescopic vision showed him to be Shadowmen emerging from Shadow Tower to intercept him.

They're troglodytes compared to us, the shadow-bite said

inside Chance's mind. They cannot begin to realize the power your strength of will has allowed us to achieve!

Chance did not waiver in his course as the Shadowmen attacked. Their strikes where useless against him, and those foolish enough to fly directly into his path collected on his outstretched arms like bugs on flypaper.

Chance focused his ichor-enshrouded eyes to allow him to see heat signatures as he continued his flight toward Shadow Tower. He immediately spotted Psy-chick and the Outlaws.

You're not going to rescue them before we have a chance to have some fun with the Shadow Prince, are you? the shadow-bite thought.

"No," Chance said, the wind swallowing his words, "he pays!"

I agree, the shadow-bite thought. *Revenge is a dish best served simmering in the blood of your enemies!*

Chance refocused his eyes so that they could actually see through Shadow Tower's walls.

"That's him!" Chance said as he shook the felled Shadow-men from his body.

Laser beams exploded from Chance's eyes. They seared a hole in Shadow Tower and surged on to strike the Shadow Prince. Mordred cringed under the attack, caught completely off-guard.

Chance zoomed inside Shadow Tower and tackled the Shadow Prince where he stood. Chance picked him up and they continued flying backward, crashing through walls.

Chance caught a glimpse of the Shadow Prince's face. He was shocked to see it was his own.

"Who—" Chance asked, "who are you?"

"Call me Mordred. It is the last name you will ever utter!"

A wave of energy exploded from Mordred's body, hurling Chance backward to crash through a series of rooms. Chance regained his footing and surged forward at superspeed. Mordred mirrored his action and they collided in the center of a large hallway. The Tower shook with the force of the crash.

But neither combatant gave quarter nor asked for it. They went at each other like dueling tornadoes, each kicking and punching with power and speed beyond human comprehension. Their battle took them in one space-time-warping-door and out another so that they struggled across every corner of the Shadow Zone.

When at last they fought their way back to Shadow Tower, they crashed through the floor and fell into the Shadow Tower's prison. Mordred knocked Chance through a wall. Chance landed and turned his head to see Psy-chick screaming at him with shocked horror.

The ichor faded from Chance's eyes. "Psy-chick?"

"Chance?"

"Enough!" Mordred yelled. He extended his hands and clouds of multicolored energy began to drain out of Chance's body into the Shadow Prince's fingertips.

No! the shadow-bite screamed inside Chance's mind. *Don't let him take our power! It's ours! Ours!*

It was over within seconds. Chance collapsed to his knees,

the shadow-bite screaming inside his mind, both of them now superpowerless.

Mordred surged forward and grabbed Chance by his throat. He tore off the Outlaw's mask and lifted him from the ground.

"You can't do this to us!" Chance screamed. "The power was ours! Ours!"

"Silence!" Mordred screamed.

Chance's mouth continued moving but it uttered no further sound.

Mordred raised his free hand. It began to glow with green energy. "Prepare to meet whatever gods you pray to!"

"No!" Psy-chick screamed.

She ran over and locked her arms around the hand Mordred was using to hold Chance.

"Please, don't!" Psy-chick pleaded. "Don't kill him!"

Mordred cocked an eyebrow. "Yet another friend for you to trouble me over, eh? Tell me, Psy-chick, why should I spare him after all the insults and indignities you have borne me?"

"I'll do anything you want! I'll be your *key*! Just don't hurt him! Please!"

"Anything? Even if it meant your death?" Mordred leaned forward so he could look Psy-chick directly in the eye. "Because it does, Psy-chick!"

Psy-chick's eyes grew wide and her bottom lip began to quiver.

"Oh, yes," Mordred said, still holding Chance at arm's length. "To open the Shadow Zone to all realities, the Vortex Chamber must spread the essence of the key to them, first."

Mordred grinned but the expression did not reach his eyes.

"I neglected to mention that minor detail, didn't I? How very forgetful of me. Perish the thought it was because I feared revealing that information to you would result in your lack of cooperation!"

"You lied to me," Psy-chick said. "All along, you were lying to me!"

"Yes, so I was," Mordred said. "And what of it? Will you play your part in my escape?" Chance squirmed as Mordred tightened his grip around the Outlaw's neck. "Or do I see how long it takes to pop your friend's eyeballs from their sockets?"

Psy-chick bowed her head. "Yes," she whispered.

"Pardon? What's that you said?"

Psy-chick raised her head and stared Mordred in the eye. "I said, 'Yes!' When the eclipse arrives, I'll be your stupid key! Just let him go."

"Certainly."

Mordred released Chance. He dropped to the floor and gasped for air, his powers of speech returned.

Mordred glided backward out of Psy-chick's cell. He waved his hand and the wall began to close up between them.

"Enjoy these final moments together with your friend, Psy-chick. I come for you in the morning."

The last of the wall closed, and the Outlaws were left alone in the dark.

37

Shocker, Space Cadet, and Viz watched Chance disappear over the horizon.

"Were you serious about someone dying?" Shocker asked.

Viz stared at the ground as she nodded.

"Are your visions ever wrong?"

"Sometimes. But not usually."

Shocker gazed skyward again to watch as the light contrail left in Chance's wake faded from view.

He briefly probed his friends' minds to gauge their mental and emotional states.

They're both pretty rattled, Shocker thought. Heck, I'm rattled! Shadow-bite or not, what the hurl was Chance thinking by flying off and leaving us? He's supposed to be our leader, flarn it!

Viz and Space Cadet looked at him, expectantly.

I guess that leaves me in the captain's chair, Shocker thought. *Well, what the hurl? There's a first time for everything!*

"We better get underground," Shocker said, "and pray that this is one of those times when your visions are wrong."

Relief showed on Viz and Space Cadet's faces. Having a leader of any caliber to steer them through the crisis was the first step toward some kind of normalcy for all concerned.

"Since lives might be on the line," Shocker said, "I say we keep moving. We won't sleep tonight, we walk. Who knows? If we get there quick enough, we still may have a chance to bring Hicksville to his senses and fix this mess."

Viz guided them to a giant tree at the marsh's edge. They entered its hollow base and continued downward inside an underground, sludge-filled tunnel leading from its roots. Eventually, the muck at their feet and along the walls gave way to the familiar hard rock crawling with bioluminescent beetles. They stopped briefly to gather a few from the wall and then pressed on.

"So what's he like?" Space Cadet asked.

"Who?" Viz replied.

"The Shadow Prince. What kind of person is he?"

"He isn't a person at all, SC," Viz said. "He's a monster."

"He can't be worse than the White Widow!"

Viz whirled and grabbed Space Cadet by his arm.

"Oh, but he can! My twin brother and I watched, helpless, as the Shadow Prince's minions kidnapped our parents. Being children of only eleven cycles, we were foolish enough to believe we could do exactly what we're attempting right now."

Viz kept talking, but her gaze was focused on some terrible, faraway memory.

"We made it a surprisingly long way—almost to Shadow Tower—but eventually they caught us. Since we were too young for our powers to have bloomed, the Shadow Prince decided to make an example of us."

Tears began to leak from Viz's eyes.

"Before turning our parents into Shadowmen, he made them use their powers to transform my brother into a ugly, deformed thing."

"What happened to you?" Space Cadet asked, his voice full of sympathy.

"The Shadow Prince let me go—forced me to go, in fact—so that I could spread the word about what would happen to anyone else stupid enough to entertain delusions about trying the same."

Viz sighed. "And yet here I am, all over again."

"It is never wrong to hope," Shocker said. "Chance taught us that, despite himself."

"Yeah," Viz said, "either I'm a romantic or a glutton for punishment!"

"If punishment is what you seek, then Ooklak say Morlock come to right place!"

The Outlaws looked up to see Ooklak and his Uruks coming out of the tunnels to surround them.

"Where little kissie boy?" Ooklak asked. "Ooklak want to punish him most of all!"

"Crap!" Shocker said. "They're so stupid I thought I was hearing the minds of cave monkeys."

"Uruks not stupid!" Ooklak raged.

"Oh yeah?" Shocker asked. "Then why are your shoes untied?"

Ooklak and the other Uruks looked down at their large, bare feet. The Outlaws leaped into action. Having a score to settle, Space Cadet went straight for Ooklak. He gave Ooklak an uppercut that knocked him into the tunnel ceiling.

"Fat one too dumb to know when he's beat!" Ooklak said as he and Space Cadet continued their battle.

"Don't call me fat!" Space Cadet yelled. He clocked Ooklak with a blow that sent the Uruk's eyes rolling in his head. "I'm pleasantly plump! Just ask my mother!"

"Plump this!" Ooklak yelled as he ripped away pieces of the rock wall and smashed them over Space Cadet's head. This time it was he who saw stars.

As SC and Ooklak fought on, Viz flowed among the other Uruks like water, gouging and beating them with her staff. They punched and kicked and reached for her, but she was too elusive and the clumsy Uruks only succeeded in hurting themselves.

"I should almost thank you Uruks," Viz said as she used her staff as a prop from which she pinwheeled her body to kick her attackers, "since the Shadow Prince isn't here for me to take my frustration out on, your showing up is a blessing in disguise!"

Nearby, Shocker used Psy-chick's psionics like an old pro. He hurled loose rocks at the Uruks with telekinesis, caused them to fight among themselves using mind control, and dodged their attacks using precognition.

"I think I'm starting to get the hang of this," he said. "It ain't quite the same as blasting, but it'll do!"

It was at this moment that everything fell apart. Space Cadet punched Ooklak so hard that he flew backward into the crowd of Uruks Viz was abusing. Viz and the Uruks tumbled like bowling pins as he impacted.

Seeing an advantage, Ooklak grabbed Viz by the throat before she could regain her composure.

"Surrender or Ooklak crush her!"

For the love of Alpha-man! Shocker thought.

"You don't want to do that," Shocker said.

"I don't want to do that," Ooklak said as though he were a puppet having his strings pulled. And that's exactly what he was—a big orange dummy for Shocker to manipulate and control with his psionics.

"You want to let her go," Shocker said.

"I want to let her go," Ooklak responded.

"In fact, you want to let us all—" Shocker felt something strike the back of the head and he fell to his knees, the tunnel spinning before his eyes.

"Me know what you doing," an Uruk said from behind Shocker. "Me bonk head and stop you!"

Ooklak shook his head and what little clarity had been there before returned to his eyes.

"What say you?" Ooklak asked.

Space Cadet raised his hands. "I give up. Just don't hurt her."

"Good," Ooklak said. He gestured to his Uruks. "Take him." They fell upon Space Cadet instantly. SC didn't fight back and it wasn't long before they carried his battered, unconscious body on their shoulders.

"No," Shocker said as he tried to struggle to his feet, "Can't let this—"

"Me say no more tricks!"

This time, Shocker didn't feel the blow. The tunnel simply went black.

38

Psy-chick bent down and placed her arms on Chance's back.

"Chance, are you all right?"

Chance abruptly stood and shook her arms from him.

"This is all your fault!" Chance fumed. "It was the sight of you that distracted us long enough for the Shadow Prince to gain the upper hand!"

"Chance," Psy-chick said, mystified, "I'm sorry, I—"

"If not for you, we'd still have our power! The power we'd always hoped and dreamed of! Now we are nothing again."

"Who's we, Chance?" Psy-chick said with concern. "What are you talking—"

Chance whirled on Psy-chick and stuck his finger in her face.

"Do you know what it feels like to command the destructive power of an atom bomb? To be stronger than a blackhole?

To soar through the sky like a rocket with only the wind between you and the ground? Huh? Do you, Psy-chick?"

"Uh, no, I—"

"It feels great!" Chance said. "In fact, it's the best feeling we've ever known. And now all because of you, it's gone! Do you understand how that makes us feel!

"Chance, I—"

"Of course you don't! You take for granted what little power you have, always showing restraint! Bowing down when those less gifted protest your abilities!"

Psy-chick crossed her arms. "God makes us strong so that we may protect the weak, Chance."

Chance turned away from her and cast his hands into the air.

"Don't hand us that Burlington textbook drivel! God makes nothing! All He does is take! And like Him, the powerful are so because they were strong enough in the first place to take from those too weak to stop them! You just saw that with your very own eyes."

"The Shadow Prince?" Psy-chick asked. "You talk as though you admire him for what he did."

"No," Chance said. "We hate him! But we will triumph. He has shown his weakness in allowing us to live."

"You would've preferred he killed you?"

"We would've killed him."

Psy-chick wagged her head as she studied Chance's back. "Who are you? What have you done with Chance Fortune?"

"Oh, it's us all right," Chance said, his voice even. "We've just grown up is all, Psy-chick. You'd be smart to do the same."

"Grown up? If it means being a ruthless, corrupted todak then I want nothing of it!"

Chance huffed.

"Chance, please." Psy-chick grabbed hold of Chance's right arm. "Turn around and talk to me."

"Don't touch us!"

Chance whipped his right arm out of Psy-chick's grasp and slapped her with the back of his hand. She cried out and then collapsed onto the cell floor.

"Psy-chick?"

Chance turned around and Psy-chick looked up at him, furious. But her anger changed into horror when she saw bubbling ichor drain from his eyes.

It's got him, she thought. *The shadow-stuff's got him!*

"Are you okay, Psy-chick? I'm so sorry."

For a moment, Chance seemed himself. But then Psy-chick noticed the capillaries in the whites of his eye changing from red to black.

"Sorry you didn't keep your hands to yourself. Look what you made us do!"

Psy-chick put her hand to her forehead. What am I going to do? The image of the lightning bolt striking the Shadow-man when she'd discovered she had Shocker's powers popped into her mind. Psy-chick recalled how the ichor had pulled away from the guard's chest where her electricity struck him. Psy-chick slowly got to her feet, knowing what she had to do.

"I'm sorry," Psy-chick said. "It was quite foolish of me to sneak up on you like that."

"Of course it was. But since you apologized, we forgive you. You are female, after all. You can't help but be foolish and unreasonable at times."

That comment almost sent a bolt of lightning charging from Psy-chick's arm. But if it struck his grounded uniform, it wouldn't do any good. She had to get close. Psy-chick cautiously walked forward.

"Chance," Psy-chick said.

"Shut up," Chance said as he examined the cell walls. "We're trying to figure a way out of here and we can't do so with your incessant prattling!"

This time, Psy-chick's hands actually began to spark with blue energy. She calmed herself and pressed on.

"Chance, really," Psy-chick said as she walked toward him, "I need to tell you—"

Chance abruptly turned and walked to the other side of the cell without looking in Psy-chick's direction.

"Tell us what?"

"It's a secret," Psy-chick said. "I need to whisper it in your ear."

"Don't be stupid," Chance said as he felt along the walls. "Anything you need to say, you can do so sounding off like a normal person!"

I swear, I'm going to kick his rear end! Psy-chick thought.

"Mordred might hear me," Psy-chick said.

"Who?"

"Mordred, the Shadow Prince. You don't want him to hear my secret, do you?"

"Is it a way out of here?" Chance asked, still not looking in Psy-chick's direction.

"Yes," Psy-chick lied, "a way out of here. That's exactly what it is."

Chance huffed and turned around. "All right. What is it you must—"

Psy-chick lunged forward, wrapped her arms around Chance, and kissed him. Little did she realize she was using his own trick against him.

Chance resisted momentarily, but whatever control the ichor held over him was not enough to suppress the magic that has existed between them. His body relaxed and he slipped his arms around her neck and waist. Then Psy-chick let him have it.

Volts of electricity passed from her lips into his. Chance had a seizure, shook and convulsed, but Psy-chick held on, refusing to let him go.

She gazed into his eyes and saw the black ooze draining away.

It's working, she thought. *I can't let up! Not until it's all gone. Every last bit of it!*

Chance's right arm straightened involuntarily so that his hand opened to the ground. Psy-chick watched in revulsion as the shadow-stuff exploded through the palm of his glove and poured onto the floor, shrieking like a wounded animal as it went, though it had no mouth.

Psy-chick waited until the very last of it drained from Chance's palm and then she released him. Chance collapsed onto his hands and knees gasping for breath. The shadow-stuff sank under the cell floor through a grate drain, its shrill screams softening and then finally petering out as it left the cell for the sewers of Shadow Tower.

Psy-chick knelt beside Chance. "Chance?"

Chance put an arm on her shoulder. "I'm OK, Psy-chick," he said as he regained his breath. "Thanks to you, I'm OK."

Psy-chick helped Chance to his knees and then they enfolded each other in their arms.

39

Shocker awoke to the pain of a throbbing headache. The world was fuzzy before his eyes and he felt numb and tingly all over.

"SC?" Shocker grunted.

"I'm right here, Shocker."

"How we doing?"

"About the same as usual."

"That bad, huh?"

"Yep."

Shocker's vision cleared and in the starlight, he saw that he, Space Cadet, and Viz were chained on top of a large, metal pedestal stationed in the center of a junkyard. The Uruks were below them, silent and hidden in the shadows among towering columns of metal debris.

"What are they doing?" Shocker asked.

"Paying tribute," Viz said, her tone deadpan.

"To who?" Space Cadet asked.

It was only then that Shocker took in the grim reality of their situation. He looked across the horizon and saw Shadow Tower rising from fields of flame to disappear among the clouds.

"It's nighttime, SC," Shocker said. "We're within miles of Shadow Tower, and the only people bullies bow down to are bigger bullies. So, in other words, who do you think?"

Space Cadet gulped as his eyes fixed on Shadow Tower.

"That's how you can stay out here so deep in the waste-lands, isn't it?" Viz yelled. "You kidnap people from other gangs and give them to the Shadowmen so they'll leave you alone, don't you, you lousy bunch of traitors!"

"Now you know truth about Uruks," Ooklak called as he peeked out from behind a pile of crushed machinery. "Not that it do little blue Morlock any good!"

Shocker strained to focus his mental abilities, trying to ignore the throbbing in his head. "You get us down from here, right now. Do you hear me?"

"Ha-ha, psychoman," one of the more weaselly-looking Uruks said. From his voice, Shocker recognized him as his head-bludgeoner. "Try harder! I mashed brain good!"

Shocker tried to focus, but it was no use. His head simply hurt too much. He cursed under his breath.

"SC," Shocker said, "can't you break us out of here?"

"I'm afraid not, Shocker. The Uruks must have constructed these chains to hold their own kind. I'm as helpless as any of them would be."

Shocker looked up and saw several dark shadows approaching fast from the direction of Shadow Tower.

"Kiss butts good-bye, little fools!" Ooklak yelled.

"Consider the floor officially open for suggestions, guys!"

"Uh," Space Cadet said, "pray?"

"Sure, SC, sure," Shocker said.

Space Cadet closed his eyes and began to pray.

"Now I lay me down to sleep—"

Shocker gritted his teeth as the red eyes of the Shadowmen became visible against the night sky.

"Well, come on then!" Shocker yelled.

"If I die before I wake—"

"Bring it on, you big ugly—"

"And I promise I'll never ever talk back to my mother—"

Loud shouts and crashes erupted in the junkyard below them.

Todaks! Shocker thought. *Dancing and celebrating while we're taken to be enslaved as mindless drones!*

The Shadowmen were now only seconds away. Shocker readied himself as three of them veered from the pack and flew directly toward them.

"I hope you rot!" Shocker yelled as the Shadowmen flew up and laid their hands on the Outlaws.

"Forever and ever, amen!"

A beam of bubbling pink plasma shot through the air and blasted the Shadowmen from the pedestal.

"Wow, pud," Shocker said in awed disbelief, "it worked!"

"Look!" Viz yelled. "The Morlocks! We're saved!"

Shocker followed her gaze downward and saw the Uruks locked in battle with the Morlocks.

Among the fray, he saw the tall, slender female who'd stood up for them in Barter Town firing blasts of the pink plasma. He scanned the faces of the combatants and realized there were many others he recognized from Barter Town.

"No," Shocker said. "Not just the Morlocks, but members from all the gangs!"

"Incredible," Viz said. "I never dreamed it possible."

"Sock it to 'em, guys!" Space Cadet called.

A series of shrieks ripped through the air and Shocker looked up to see the rest of the Shadowmen streaking through the sky toward them.

The Outlaws squirmed against their chains, but to no avail. Several Shadowmen broke off to enter the battle below. The remainder landed on the pedestal. Their eyes and hands began to power up with energy as they readied to strike.

"Brutus!" Viz called.

The Morlock strongman leaped on top of the pedestal and knocked the Shadowmen from their perch.

"What are we? Chopped liver?"

The bat-boy flew up to join them. He carried a green-skinned girl by his feet. She chanted an unintelligible spell and the Outlaws' chains fell away.

"Thanks," Shocker said. "We owe you!"

Viz and Brutus embraced. He pulled away and turned his back to her. He removed his cloak to reveal Caesar's wrinkled, oversized head.

"Oo," Space Cadet said, "gross!"

Shocker slapped him on the back.

"Sorry!"

"Better to meet destiny on your feet," Caesar said to Viz, "than cowering in a cave."

Viz nodded.

"That sounds like something Chance would say," Space Cadet said.

Viz turned to him. "That's because he did."

"And I'm glad of it," Caesar said. "We left Morlock City shortly after you did, gathering support along the way. The gangs have declared a tenuous truce. It seems they were as tired of living under the Shadow Prince's thumb as we were."

"Attaboy!" Shocker said as he patted Brutus's shoulder.

He leaped onto Space Cadet's back. "Well, come on, pud. Let's not let them steal all the fun!"

"Right!"

Space Cadet leaped from the pedestal and sent a horde of Shadowmen and Uruks tumbling to the ground as he and Shocker landed in the basin below. Viz and the others quickly joined them. But by the time they got there, the battle was practically over and all that was left to do was mop up.

"Piece of cake," Space Cadet said as he dropped a final unconscious Shadowman and wiped his hands.

"This was just a hunting party," the tall girl said. "The Shadow Prince's full army will not fall so easy."

"You prove what we Morlocks have always said about the Gladiatrices, Isis," Mace said as his hands transformed into weapons. "You are cowards, and cannot be trusted!"

Pink plasma bubbled in Isis's eyes as several other females from her gang gathered around her.

"Skulking Morlock!" Isis said. "Always acting superior!"

"We'll show you just how superior we are!" the bat-boy said as he and many other Morlocks joined Mace at his side.

The two sides began shouting and yelling at each other. Feuds broke out among several more groups and before long the entire basin was in a clamor once again.

"This isn't good," Space Cadet said.

"So loud." Shocker put his hands to his aching head. "Can't you all just be *QUIET!*"

The entire basin fell into silence. The gang members looked at one another in fear as they struggled and failed to open their mouths.

Shocker hopped up onto a small pile of debris.

"OK, listen up and listen good!" Shocker said. He also projected his words directly into the gang members' minds for added emphasis. "I'm not good at giving inspirational speeches. That's my captain's bag. But he's not here, and I'm all you've got.

"How many of you have family and friends who the Shadow Prince has stolen from you?"

The gang members looked at one another.

"Go ahead," Shocker said as he released them from his psychic hold. "How many?"

Every hand in the basin went up.

"That's right! All of us! A week ago, he took the people who mean the most to me in the entire world! I've been nothing but scared and heartbroken since."

Shocker hopped down and began to walk among the crowd.

"But even more than that, I've been angry. I'm angry that anyone thinks they have the right to step on the innocent! I'm angry someone thinks they can take what they want without regard for anyone or anything!

"You all are obviously angry, too, or you wouldn't be here. Well, I say nothing's changed. The choice is still yours!

"Will you set aside your petty differences and go save your friends? Or will you continue to squabble among yourselves while the Shadow Prince laughs at you from his tower?"

A large, insectoid superhuman carrying ancient weapons in all of his six arms stepped forward. Two furry antennae sprouted from his head above several pairs of eyes. In place of his mouth sat a fearsome mandible that looked like it could crush a human femur with ease. He clicked and chirped several unintelligible sounds and then the insect-boy began to speak.

"I am Kaphka, of the Buggers. Who are you who speaks so?"

"I'm called Shocker. What of it?"

"What gang are you from?"

"The best, though we're a team, not a gang. I'm an Outlaw."

Kaphka pressed his weaponed fists to his segmented chest in salute.

"Today, we are all Outlaws!"

Kaphka threw his arms into the air and began to cheer. The crowd soon joined in.

"Outlaws! Outlaws! Outlaws!"

"Not bad for someone who doesn't like to give speeches," Viz remarked with a smile.

"Yes," Shocker said. "Now please excuse me while I go throw up."

40

Chance and Psy-chick released each other and sat back against the cell wall.

"And here I thought I was supposed to be rescuing you," Chance said.

"Let's see that hand," Psy-chick said.

Chance held his right hand out to Psy-chick. She took it in her own. She gently removed what remained of his tattered glove and examined his palm. A dark, jagged scar ran down its length.

"It looks like a jagged S," Chance said.

"Or the Burlington emblem," Psy-chick said.

"So it does."

"Can you make a fist?"

Chance slowly closed his hand.

"Can you squeeze it any tighter?"

"No, a loose grip is the best I can do."

"That's a pretty bad wound, Chance. It may never heal properly."

"I feared as much."

Chance pressed his back against the wall and his feet against the floor as he lifted his hips. Braced there, he undid his utility belt and shifted his grappling gun to his left side. He sat back down and finished fastening the holster to his left leg.

"Mom said it took me forever to make up my mind which would be my dominant hand, anyway."

"What was it like, Chance?"

"What do you mean?"

"All that power at your fingertips."

"It was . . . corruptive. And far too much for any one person to have."

Even as Chance spoke, his face was full of longing. But he turned and looked Psy-chick in the eye and it passed. He placed his left hand in her's.

"Thank you, Psy. You pulled me back from the abyss. I owe you my life."

"You would've done the same for me and more, Chance."

Both their cheeks reddened and they looked away from each other. A moment later, Psy-chick's eyes grew wide with excitement.

"Oh!" she said. "Shocker? SC? Are they—"

"Also alive, and well on their way here to rescue you and the others when I left them."

Psy-chick breathed a sigh of relief and sagged against the wall.

"What are we going to do, Chance?"

Chance looked at her and had to stop tears from welling in his eyes.

Be strong for her, he thought.

"We'll figure something out," Chance told her, hoping he sounded more confident than he felt.

"I know we will," Psy-chick said. "We've got your luck on our side, after all."

They sat in silence for several moments.

I'm going to do it, Chance thought. *I'm going to tell her I'm only human. If these are to be our last hours together, I don't want any secrets between us.*

"Psy-chick, there's something I need to tell you . . . something I should've told you a long time ago."

"What is it, Chance?"

Chance began to pace the cell.

"Whatever it is, Chance, you can tell me."

Chance chuckled but his laughter did not reach his eyes.

"Oh, I don't know about this one, Psy."

"It can't be that big a deal."

"Oh, it's pretty big. Especially considering our situation. Pretty big indeed!"

"Well, OK. Go on, then."

"You know how sometimes," Chance said as he paced and gesticulated, "you can want something so bad, it seems as though you'd do anything to get it?"

Psy-chick cocked her eyebrows in question.

"Or how your heart's desire can be right there in front of you, but just out of reach," Chance continued, "and to get it, you do things you normally wouldn't do? Say things you normally wouldn't say? Act in ways you normally wouldn't act?

Psy-chick got to her feet and smiled.

"What I'm trying to say is," Chance said, "that there comes a time when you have to lay it all out on the line. You just have to go for it, regardless of the consequences, because you know it will be the greatest thing to ever happen to you."

Psy-chick walked over to Chance and took his hands in hers.

"And you've just got to—"

Psy-chick pressed her finger to Chance's lips, shushing him.

"It's OK, Chance. I feel the same way."

Psy-chick leaned in and kissed Chance. His eyes went wide with surprise and stayed that way until she released him.

"That's the first time I've ever kissed a girl, Psy-chick. I mean a *real* kiss."

"No kidding?"

Chance shrugged. "I guess in my quest to be Burlington's best student, I've missed a lot, huh?"

"It was nice."

"Really?"

"Yeah."

"Can we do it again?" Chance asked, now smiling.

Psy-chick grinned and leaned into him once more. This time, Chance took to it more easily and wrapped his arms around her.

Their mouths parted but they remained in each other's

arms. They stayed that way through the night, talking and even laughing as they spoke of home, family, and friends. Their bond was an impenetrable sanctuary against the shadow of evil that surrounded them.

It was only with the approach of dawn that their conversation turned to grimmer subjects.

"That sounds like a good plan, Psy-chick," Chance said after hearing what Psy-chick wanted to do with Mordred. "And I know just how to get it started."

Chance produced a smoke-colored bulb from his utility belt.

"This is my last UV flare," Chance said. "It's toxic to the Shadowmen. When they come for us, I will ignite it and try to hold them off long enough for you to make your escape."

"You're taking an awful big risk," Psy-chick said. "Can't we stun them with the flare and then flee?"

Chance shook his head.

"The Shadow Prince would find us anywhere we went. You said so yourself."

Psy-chick nodded reluctantly.

"All right. So when they—"

Chance jerked his head around toward the door and listened.

"Footsteps! They're here! Get ready to run."

The cell door changed into a mass of ichor and peeled itself open. Three Shadowmen stood outside the cell. They beckoned for Psy-chick to come forward.

"I don't think so!" Chance said and smashed the UV flare against the floor. It ignited in a brilliant burst of white light that illuminated the cell interior. The Shadowmen recoiled, shrieking as the ichor coating their bodies went into fits.

Psy-chick blasted one with a bolt of lightning as Chance dispatched the other two with punches and kicks.

Chance was about to grab Psy-chick's hand and run when he felt someone seize the back of his neck.

"I thought as much," Mordred said from behind him.

The world became a blur before Chance's eyes as Mordred effortlessly tossed him back into his cell.

"Psy-chick!" Chance yelled.

He watched as a cocoon of shadow enveloped Psy-chick and Mordred and lifted them into the ceiling before the cell door closed.

41

Shocker, Space Cadet, and Viz stood on top of a giant boulder watching the last sliver of sun rise behind Shadow Tower. The Shadow Zone gangs stood below them in formation, awaiting Shocker's command to attack. After a night-long discussion of strategy with the gang leaders, it had been decided that Shocker would serve as battle commander, if for no other reason than to maintain harmony among all the factions. His psionic abilities went a long way to help in that regard.

Why did the march here have to be over so fast? Shocker thought. *Flarn you, Hicksville! It's supposed to be you up here leading the revolt against the forces of evil, not some smart-mouth kid from the Megalopolis ghettos!*

"Freezers!" Shocker barked. He also projected his words mentally. "Take out those flames. I want a winter wonderland all the way to Shadow Tower!"

The gang members with cold powers stepped forward and

let loose a torrent of ice, wind, and snow over the horse-head pumps and the flames they produced. The flames were snuffed and the pumps frozen solid within seconds.

"When the sun goes into full eclipse," Viz said, "we're going to have a world of hurt on our hands."

"We'll be fine so long as everyone sticks to the plan," Shocker said.

"I hope you're right," Viz said.

"We're about to find out," Space Cadet said.

The three of them looked on in silence as the moons' dark silhouette eclipsed the last of the sun. Darkness fell and Shadowmen immediately began to pour out of the Tower.

"Air force," Shocker said, "get up there. High. Stay away from direct fighting if you can, but keep us covered."

Young superhumans of all descriptions flew into the sky under the power of wing, flame, and levitation to disappear into the clouds.

"They're coming fast," Space Cadet said.

"There must be thousands of them," Viz said, her voice wavering.

The approaching horde of Shadowmen looked like an inky blanket spread across the already darkened sky. Shocker felt a wave of panic course through the gangs as the shrieking battle cries of the Shadowmen began to fill the air.

"Steady, Outlaws!" Shocker yelled as he used Psychick's powers of empathy to radiate confidence. "Hold your ground!"

The Shadowmen began to glow as those with energy abilities charged them up.

"Steady, now!" Shocker yelled. "Wait until you can see the whites, uh, reds of their eyes!"

The Shadowmen's Supreme General flew out ahead of his army, his face forming into a proboscis as he closed in on Shocker. He seemed to perceive Shocker's role as the resistance leader.

"Hold," Shocker yelled. "Hold!"

Shocker reached inside his jacket pocket as the Shadowman neared him.

"Smile, you son of—"

Shocker withdrew a jar of the bioluminescent beetles from his jacket and thrust it out at the General. The Shadowman shrieked in pain and fear and then crashed at Shocker's feet. Viz stepped up and used her bo staff to send the General into dreamland.

"Now, Outlaws!" Shocker screamed. "Now!"

All around them, hundreds of young superhumans lifted jars of shining beetles into the air. The hordes of Shadowmen reacted the same as their General. They shrieked in agony and tumbled from the sky to the ground.

"Let 'em have it!" Shocker yelled.

Laser beams and horizontal jets of flame crisscrossed the battlefield, striking Outlaw and Shadowman alike. Lightning pounded down upon them from the heavens and the earth quaked beneath their feet. Hurricane blasts of wind blew the combatants around like autumn leaves and giant, fiery explosions billowed into the sky.

Space Cadet and Viz knocked away any Shadowmen who dared step onto Shocker's rock command post.

"Let's move," Shocker said.

Space Cadet nodded. He hooked his arm around Shocker's waist and leaped off the boulder. Viz jumped down after them, swatting away two Shadowmen as she landed.

"Isis!" Shocker called. "Clear us a path!"

Seconds later, Isis appeared and began to blaze a trail through the Shadowmen with blasts of bubbling pink plasma from her hands. Shocker, Space Cadet, and Viz followed behind her as she advanced across the frost-covered plane for Shadow Tower.

They were halfway there when a hulking Shadowman pressed his way through the crowd and knocked Isis from her feet. The Shadowman was raising his fists to finish her off when he halted in his tracks and fell forward onto his face.

Mace stood behind the Shadowman's unconscious body. He extended a spiked fist to Isis and helped her to her feet.

"Don't think this means I like you!" Mace growled.

Isis frowned and fired a plasma bolt in Mace's direction. He ducked just in time for the blast to miss him. It struck a Shadowman who had been sneaking up on Mace from behind, putting him out of commission.

"That goes double for me!" Isis said.

They grinned at each other and then continued clearing the way to Shadow Tower.

Several blasts, kicks, punches, and swats later, the Outlaws reached their destination.

"I need an ice bridge over that moat," Shocker yelled. "On the double!"

Two superhumans, one a Little Coffin Hunter, the other a

Fast Mutant, lifted their hands and crystallized the moisture in the air above the moat to form a plank of ice that stretched from shore to shore.

As Shocker and a crowd of others raced over it, a gigantic ichor monster burst out of the moat and roared. It opened its massive jaws and struck at them like a cobra. A right-cross from Space Cadet sent it retreating back into the depths.

"Specs!" Shocker called.

The Morlock stepped forward. "Yes, Shocker?"

"Does this thing have a weak point? Somewhere we can blast our way in?"

Specs put a hand to his glasses and looked the tower up and down.

"There!" he said as he pointed to a spot several stories up.

"Light it up, Isis," Shocker said.

An especially large beam of plasma rocketed out of Isis's hands to strike the Tower in the spot identified by Specs. Several other teens with similar powers joined their energy to hers and, at last, a gaping hole appeared in the side of Shadow Tower.

"Tiny," Shocker called, "you're up!"

A towering, preteen giant came across the ice bridge and lowered his hands so that Shocker, Space Cadet, and Viz could climb onto them. Tiny lifted them to the entrance the blasters had blown open in Shadow Tower's side. They leaped from his hand inside.

"Keep them busy out here, Tiny," Shocker said. "I'll call for you to transport more once we've secured things a bit inside."

The giant nodded and then rejoined the battle raging outside Shadow Tower.

Shocker and the others turned to see Shadowmen spilling onto the floor they'd breached.

"For Iron Maiden and Psy-chick!" Shocker yelled.

"For Gothika and PJ!" SC added.

"For my family!" Viz said.

The Outlaws charged forward to attack, unaware one of them would fail to survive the day.

42

Psy-chick struggled in Mordred's grasp as the shadow cocoon writhed around them.

"Let me go!" She shouted.

"Be still!" Mordred commanded. "You agreed to this."

Mordred's eyes flashed and all the strength drained out of Psy-chick.

"But you're going to kill me!"

"A liar and a welcher until the end, then, eh, Psy-chick?"

"You're a monster!"

Mordred smiled facetiously. "No, simply misunderstood."

The shadow cocoon peeled away and Psy-chick saw that they were in the Vortex Chamber at Shadow Tower's apex. The walls spun madly around them. Dr. Faustoid stood hunched over a holographic interface making final adjustments.

"We are here, Faustoid," Mordred said.

Dr. Faustoid whirled to face them.

"Yes!" Faustoid cried. His hands glided over a series of holograms and the pedestal control panel at the room's center dropped to become level to the floor.

Mordred dragged Psy-chick over to it.

"Why are you doing this, Mordred? I would've been your friend!"

"I told you," Mordred exclaimed as he shoved Psy-chick onto the pedestal's top, "I have no need of friends. I will be free this day!"

"Mordred, please!"

"Why can't you understand, Psy-chick? I have to do this!"

"No you don't!"

"Yes, I do. My father's reign of tyranny over the multiverse must come to an end!"

"Only so that you may take his place!"

"And would that be so horrible? My father demands total obedience. He gives his subjects no choice as to how they wish to live their lives. I would free them from that. I would give them the choice my father denies them."

"And what of your Shadowmen? Did they have a choice?"

"You have such a limited grasp of the matter, Psy-chick. Since the beginning of time, every nation of freedom has been built upon the backs of those who had none.

"No! That's not true! God makes us strong so that we may protect the weak, not bully them!"

Mordred studied Psy-chick, pity in his eyes. "Forgive me, Psy-chick. You are not a liar. Merely naïve to a fault."

"Master!" Dr. Faustoid called. "The eclipse is upon us!"

The Shadow Prince stepped back and a cage of black steel rose from the floor and encased her. The six posts rose into place and a hole opened in the ceiling's center to reveal the moons' shadow covering the last gleaming edge of the sun.

Psy-chick's pedestal-prison began to rise from the floor. Bolts of green lightning discharged from the posts and struck her cage. The energy ran up and down its length as though her cell were a Tesla coil.

"At long last," Mordred said as he raised his hands in exaltation, "freedom!"

Psy-chick closed her eyes. She was going to die and there was no way to stop it.

Psy-chick's life passed before her eyes. She thought of her childhood in Mexico. She saw her mother's soft, glowing face and smelled her jasmine-scented perfume. She felt her father's strong, coarse hands as he tossed her playfully into the air so that she would squeal with glee before he caught her again. She warmed inside as she roughhoused with her three older brothers all over again and then smiled when her mind's eye saw the tall, lanky protectors they had grown up to be.

At last, her mind turned to Chance and the night they'd shared talking and laughing as they'd held each other. Despite the looming of death's shadow, or perhaps because of it, that was her favorite memory of all. As Psy-chick played it over in her mind, she felt her strength return.

Psy-chick heard the sizzle of electricity peter out. She opened her eyes and saw Dr. Faustoid frantically working at the Vortex Chamber's controls.

"What is it, Faustoid?" Mordred spat. "What's wrong? Why is it not working?"

"I'm checking, master," Dr. Faustoid said. "Everything appears in order. Everything checks out. I—"

Mordred zipped across the room at superspeed and grabbed Dr. Faustoid by his throat. He lifted him into the air.

"I swear, Faustoid," Mordred fumed, "if you have failed me I'll—"

"I've not failed you, master," Dr. Faustoid said, choking out the words, "the Vortex Chamber is fully operational."

"Then what is the meaning of this? Why is the dimensional barrier still in place?"

"We don't have adequate power, master."

Mordred's eyes narrowed. "What do you mean, we don't have adequate—"

Mordred released Dr. Faustoid and the technomancer fell to the floor. He lay there gasping for air and clutching at his cybernetic throat.

Mordred's head slowly turned in Psy-chick's direction. When their eyes locked, Psy-chick saw death—her death.

Mordred waved his hand and the cage imprisoning Psy-chick opened. Using his powers of levitation, Mordred lifted Psy-chick out of the cage and brought her over to hang in the air before him.

"That was no jest you told on your first night here, was it?" Mordred spat. "You have lost your psionic abilities, haven't you?"

"Yeah," Psy-chick said, "but I've learned some new tricks!"

Lightning leaped from Psy-chick's eyes and struck Mordred in the chest. The Shadow Prince flinched as though he'd been bitten by a mosquito and then shrugged it off.

"That tickled," Mordred said. "It will take a lot more than that to hurt me. Let's see if the same can be said of you."

Mordred raised his hand and Psy-chick screamed as pain began pulsing through her body.

Anger consumed Mordred. "I will make your suffering last for aeons! I will—"

The Vortex Chamber shook as though a bomb had exploded somewhere within Shadow Tower. Alarms began to wail and sirens began to flash.

"Master!" Dr. Faustoid, now on his feet again, called. "The Tower has been breached!"

"No doubt that's my friends—the friends you thought were dead—coming to pay you a visit," Psy-chick said. "Surprise!"

Mordred scowled at Psy-chick. He dropped her and his body swelled, morphing into its true ichor-geyser form. It spiraled upward to the ceiling, its giant coils of liquid shadow filling the chamber before surging downward to disappear through the floor.

With the pain leaving her body, Psy-chick leaped to her feet. Lightning shot from her hands only to bounce harmlessly off the Vortex Chamber's controls.

They've put up a force field, Psy-chick thought. My zaps are useless! I'll have to go to Plan B.

Psy-chick bolted for the door.

"Where do you think you're going?" Dr. Faustoid said as he grabbed Psy-chick with a steely black claw.

Psy-chick sent several volts surging up his arm and he shrieked as circuits blew all over his body. When Psy-chick stopped, Dr. Faustoid fell to the floor, unconscious, his body smoking where it lay.

Tommie, here I come!

43

Chance pounded his fists against his cell door.

"Let me out of here!"

Suddenly, the ground shook as something exploded within Shadow Tower and Chance fell to the floor.

"What the hurl?"

Chance got to his feet and resumed banging on his cell door.

"What's going on out there? Let me out, right now! Do you hear me?"

"Ribbit hear you. *Ribbit.*"

Chance stepped back, dumbstruck to have his pleas answered.

"Hello?" Chance asked. "Who's out there?"

"Ribbit out here. *Ribbit.* Ribbit come to free Pretty Girl. Is Pretty Girl in there?"

"Pretty Girl? Who is—Oh, you must mean Psy-chick."

"Yes. *Ribbit*. Pretty Girl!"

"She was in here, but the Shadow Prince took her."

"Shadow Prince hurt Ribbit. *Ribbit*. Shadow Prince very bad."

"Please, I need you to let me out. I've got to save Psy-chick before he can . . . hurt her. Will you help me?"

Chance stood in silence for a moment, waiting for an answer.

"I said, will you—"

Chance's cell door peeled away. He saw a misshapen creature holding one of the Shadowmen's arms on the other side. The creature was froglike and its left arm hung in a makeshift splint and sling.

At the sight of Chance, it dropped the Shadowman's arm and began to scurry backward in fear.

He thinks I'm Mordred.

Chance held up his hands, palms out.

"No, wait. I'm not the Shadow Prince. I'm a good guy . . . a friend."

The frog-boy halted and tilted its head in question.

"Ribbit's friend? Like Pretty Girl? *Ribbit*."

"Yes, I'm your friend, uh, Ribbit. Look—"

Chance took an auxiliary mask out of his utility belt and tied it on.

"The Shadow Prince is gone. Only friends here. Will you help me save Psy-chick?"

Ribbit approached cautiously.

"Ribbit help. Pretty Girl Ribbit's friend. *Ribbit*."

"Good! Do you know where they are?"

"Who? *Ribbit.*"

"Psy-chick and the Shadow Prince. Do you know where he's taken her?"

Ribbit pointed at the ceiling. "Up!"

"Up where, Ribbit?"

"Up! *Ribbit.* To very tip-top!"

Banging sounded from behind the cell doors.

"Chance? Is that you out there?"

"Justice?"

"Let us out!"

"Ribbit," Chance said, "those are Psy-chick's friends, too. Can you free them like you did me?"

Ribbit nodded and then took the still sleeping Shadowman's arm back in his. He waved it at the cell doors housing the Outlaws. They opened and Gothika, Iron Maiden, and Private Justice came running out. They enveloped Chance in a bear hug.

"Chance," Gothika said, "you're alive!"

"Odin be praised!" Iron Maiden said.

"We'll celebrate later," Chance said. "Right now, Psy-chick is in terrible danger!"

"What are your orders, Chance?" Private Justice said.

"Come," Ribbit said, "Ribbit take you! *Ribbit.*"

Ribbit bounded across the cell block and up the winding staircase leading out of it. The Outlaws chased after him. They'd cleared several floors when a group of Shadowmen came crashing through a wall. The Outlaws turned and braced themselves, ready to fight them off. But as the Shadowmen flew by, Chance noticed their bodies were spinning through the air.

They didn't fly through the wall, Chance thought. *They were thrown!*

Chance looked through the gaping hole left in the Shadowmen's wake.

"SC?"

Space Cadet turned, his fist held ready to punch.

"Chance? Gothika! Maiden! PJ!"

A horde of Shadowmen flew through the air and tackled Space Cadet.

Chance leaped through the hole just in time to see Space Cadet burst out from under the Shadowmen piled on top of him. Chance cringed as the discarded Shadowmen hurtled through the air toward him. Gothika snaked her elastic body in front of Chance and spread it out like a blanket. The Shadowmen bounced harmlessly off of her.

Chance felt a hand grab his shoulder. He spun around, throwing his momentum into his left fist. Viz caught his hand in her own just as he was about to clock her. Shocker stood beside her, a grin spread across his face.

"Shocker!" Iron Maiden cried. She charged forward and wrapped him in her arms.

"Good to see you, too, Red."

He released her and high-fived Private Justice. Gothika rejoined them, her elongated arm wrapped around Space Cadet's shoulder.

"Sister?" Ribbit said.

"Vox!" Viz said.

"Sister!"

Ribbit hopped over and leaped into Viz's arms.

"Thank the Old Ones," Viz said. "I was afraid I'd never see you again!"

"Looks like the gang's all here," Shocker said.

"Guys," Chance said, "we've got to get to the top of Shadow Tower and save Psy-chick. There's not a second to—"

At that moment, a giant ball of ichor unfurled from the ceiling's shadows and landed among them. A wave of energy discharged from it in all directions and knocked the Outlaws to the ground. As they lay there, the ichor changed shape into the Shadow Prince's Chance-like form.

"Mordred!" Chance said.

"You," Mordred spat.

Mordred roared and his body darkened and swelled until it touched the ceiling. Mordred now stood in his true form— a giant, black monster of ichor. His arms and legs were tree trunks of molten shadow and the single crimson eye in his globular head blazed with rage and hatred.

The glow in Mordred's eye increased in intensity and Chance rolled out of the way just in time to dodge the beam of energy that came lasering out of it. The beam burned through the floor and several more beneath it.

Viz hurled her bo staff through the air like a spear. It struck Mordred square in the eye. He winced and stumbled backward, the pounding of his steps shaking the room.

"Outlaws, attack!" Chance said. "Everything you've got! Don't give him a second to breathe!"

Gothika stretched forward and wrapped her body around

Mordred's giant ichor legs. Space Cadet charged forward like a bull and knocked the already off-balance Shadow Prince to the ground.

Gothika and Space Cadet moved out of the way as Private Justice stepped forward and chanted a spell. He brought the ceiling crashing down on top of Mordred.

The pile of debris trembled and then finally exploded outward to reveal Mordred's unshaped mass. The Shadow Prince slithered around the room like a living tidal wave, knocking Outlaws left and right. Mordred washed over Chance and scooped him into the air, forming his monstrous shape around the Outlaw so that he held Chance within a giant fist. Mordred began to squeeze and Chance cried out.

Shocker sent pieces of rubble hurling through the air with his mind. They slammed into Mordred, driving him backward.

"Chance, here!" Viz called. She tossed a jar of beetles through the air. Chance caught it and held it up directly before Mordred's cyclopean eye. The Shadow Prince howled with rage and pain as he lost his shape and dropped Chance to the ground.

Mordred gathered himself and wormed across the room at incredible speed toward Shocker. He took on his Chance-husk as he seized Shocker by the throat.

Mordred tightened his grip and Shocker gasped for air. Then, suddenly, Mordred halted. His eyes flashed as he scanned Shocker at the subatomic level.

"The key!" Mordred said.

He enveloped them in a cocoon of shadow that rocketed upward to disappear through the ceiling.

"No!" Chance screamed.

Shadowmen poured into the room from the hole left in the ceiling. Chance rolled out of their way, separating himself from the others.

"Come!" Ribbit shouted. He stood at a staircase on Chance's side of the room, beckoning to him.

"Go ahead, Chance," Iron Maiden shouted as she whacked a Shadowman across the head with a piece of rubble. "Save them! We'll catch up as soon as we can!"

Without hesitation, Chance turned and bolted up the staircase. Ribbit was already on the move ahead of him.

"Please," Chance said as he took the stairs three at a time, "don't let me be too late!"

44

The shadow cocoon opened and Shocker saw that they were in a spinning room. The revolving walls traded zaps of green electricity with a black steel cage in the room's center.

"Faustoid," Mordred said, "I have the key. The real one!" Mordred waved his hand and Dr. Faustoid lifted from the ground, his body as good as new.

"Hurry, master," Dr. Faustoid said. "Place him into the Vortex Chamber power cell. The eclipse is almost over!"

Still holding Shocker by the throat, Mordred slithered across the room and slammed the Outlaw into the cage. It clanged shut around him.

Shocker grimaced as he sent mind bullets hurtling at the Shadow Prince.

Mordred howled. "Stay out of my head, mortal!" He hurled a ball of red energy through the cage. It struck Shocker and knocked him backward before fading away.

"*Now, Faustoid,*" Mordred screamed. "*Now!*"

Dr. Faustoid maneuvered his hand over the holographic controls. The cage began to rise toward the ceiling. The green lightning increased in volume and intensity until it filled the chamber.

Then sound, energy, and motion imploded to the size of a pinpoint somewhere deep within Shocker, leaving the outside world still and silent.

Shocker exhaled all the air from his lungs. The world restarted as a continuous beam of crackling green energy exploded upward from the pedestal. The beam passed through Shocker and struck the sky where shadow covered the eclipsed sun.

Shocker felt his inner self being carried upward along with it. He felt the beam blast against some invisible barrier that cracked under its onslaught. As the fissure widened, Shocker felt his essence pour out over countless worlds, galaxies, and universes. He felt a part of himself within everything from the tiniest grain of sand to the stormy, nuclear heart of the multiverse's brightest burning star.

"All of it at once," Shocker mumbled, "so beautiful. If only everyone could see it this way."

"The wormhole has become self-sustaining, master," Dr. Faustoid said. "Shall I deactivate the Vortex Chamber?"

"You're certain the wormhole has fully stabilized?" Mordred asked.

Dr. Faustoid nodded.

"As you will, then."

Dr. Faustoid manipulated the holographic controls and

the beam of energy blinked out of existence. Shocker's cage sank back to the floor as the spinning walls slowed and the green lightning ceased crisscrossing the room.

Mordred waved his hand and the cage opened. Shocker fell out of it onto the ground. His breathing was slow and his eyes stared far off at some wonderment known only to him.

"And now I will bid this wretched place good-bye!" Mordred said. His torso changed into an ichor mass that began to stretch toward the opening in the ceiling.

At that moment, Chance and Ribbit burst through the Vortex Chamber's entrance.

"Shocker!" Chance yelled.

"Don't bother with me, Chance," Shocker said. "Stop him! Do what you must!"

"Master!" Dr. Faustoid cried.

Ribbit leaped at the technomancer, knocked him to the floor, and sat there upon his chest, pinning him to the ground.

"Master, save me!"

"Of what concern are you to me, fool?" Mordred said.

His body coiled upon itself until he stood as a near-mirror image of Chance.

"However, I will gladly let the death of these two be my final act in this accursed dimension."

Mordred approached Chance as though he had all the time in the world.

"I should have done this a long time ago, human."

Chance's eyes widened, but he stood his ground.

"That's right," Mordred said. "I know of your normalcy.

I've known since the first time my minion scanned your DNA at Burlington Academy.

He must mean Legion, Chance thought. *The monster didn't bother trying to possess me because I was only human.*

"You are a liar and a fraud!" Mordred continued. "You feign strength and confidence, but it is all an act. You have no superpowers at all. Not anymore."

Mordred grinned with a crocodile's smile as he gestured to Chance's uniform.

"And that's what this is all about, isn't it? All this playacting? You hide behind that costume and that mask so that no one will realize what an incompetent buffoon you really are."

Mordred crossed his arms and studied Chance's face.

"Or does your neurosis go even further than that? Is the time you've wasted at Burlington Academy—and even before then, all those years you spent training with that old fool in his backyard—is that some sort of self-induced penance?"

Chance took a backward step.

"Why that's it, isn't it?" Mordred said, his eyes alive with excitement. "Even though he's been dead and gone for years, you're still trying to save daddy!"

"You shut up!" Chance said. "You shut your mouth, right now!"

"Yes, I know all about your life in Littleton," Mordred laughed, "including your father's suicide. Thankfully, Dr. Faustoid has sources of information other than the Burlington Academy databases."

Mordred shook his head.

"What a strange specimen you are! Your guilt is groundless

and yet it has shaped every decision you've ever made. You carry on, convincing yourself you can save your father though you are totally and utterly powerless to do so!"

"I said shut up!"

"Now, calm down, human. I find your powers of complete self-delusion amusing. It gives me an idea . . . instead of killing you, what if I was to help you?"

Chance stepped forward. "What do you mean?"

"What if I told you it was within my power to grant you what it is you seek?"

"You can bring my father back?" Chance asked, dumbstruck.

"Don't listen to him, Chance," Shocker whispered. "He is the prince of shadows and deception. His words are lies."

"Quiet, fool!" Mordred barked. Then his smile returned.

"So what do you say?" Mordred closed the remaining distance between them. "Shall I return the father that fear and despair took from you?"

Chance looked to Shocker and then back to Mordred. After an eternity-long moment of silence, he spoke.

"I already have a father. And he is Fearless!"

Chance ripped his jar of beetles from a compartment in his utility belt and pressed it against Mordred's face. The Shadow Prince screamed in agony as his skin sizzled under its shining light.

Mordred collapsed onto his hands and knees and scampered across the room, the jar-shaped brand over his right eye still smoking.

Chance charged after him and grabbed hold of Mordred's

gelatinous bulk as it began to stretch for the opening in the ceiling. Chance lifted the jar to thrust against Mordred's side. A laser beam from the Shadow Prince's remaining eye struck it, shattering the glass and scattering the beetles so that their light diminished considerably.

Mordred fell upon Chance and resumed the Outlaw's shape. But he was unable to transform the skin that had melted over his eye beneath the beetle shine.

"Now you die, human!" Mordred screamed. He raised his fist and it transformed into a gigantic mass of hammer-shaped ichor.

Mordred was just about to bring the appendage crashing down on Chance's head when the Shadow Prince screamed in pain and toppled off of him. The Shadow Prince sat there panting as he grabbed at his chest.

His face turned into a scowl. "Psy-chick!"

Mordred's body collapsed into a mass of ichor that sank into the floor.

45

Psy-chick soared through the darkened sky on the great red dragon's back.

"Look, Tommie," Psy-chick said as she pointed toward Shadow Tower. Its apex rose out of a cloud bank in the distance. "Almost there. We better descend."

Tommie roared and dropped beneath the clouds. The air was filled with the thunderous din of war. Young superhumans were battling Shadowmen everywhere. She and the dragon were immediately surrounded by airborne explosions. Tommie looped and banked, dodging stray lasers and energy beams.

Psy-chick heard a scream and looked down to see a pack of flying Shadowmen blasting away with force-pulses and lightning bolts as they chased the bat-boy and an angel-winged girl.

"Tommie," Psy-chick said as she tightened her grip on the dragon, "there, dive!"

Tommie obeyed and furled his wings. He and Psy-chick dropped like a stone through the air, the wind whistling in their ears. At the last second, the dragon spread his leathery wings to their full and considerable span so that they leveled off directly behind the Shadowmen.

Tommie roared and the Shadowmen looked back to peer at him with stupefied disbelief. The dragon let loose a torrent of flame from its throat that scattered them in all directions.

"Thanks for the save," the bat-boy said as he and the winged girl came to fly alongside them.

"Don't mention it!" Psy-chick said. "From what Chance tells me, we owe you!

"Where are Shocker and the others?"

"They are in the tower," the bat-boy said, "looking for you, actually."

"What?" Psy-chick asked.

"They infiltrated Shadow Tower to help you escape," the bat-boy said. "But it looks like you beat them to it!"

"In the tower?" Psy-chick said. "Oh, no! That's exactly what Mordred would want."

"Who?"

"Never mind. How long have they been in there?"

"Not long. Maybe twenty minutes at the most."

"Maybe there's still time," Psy-chick said. "I have to act quickly!"

"Is there anything we can do to help?" the winged girl asked.

"You're already doing it," Psy-chick said. "Keep as many of the Shadowmen engaged out here as possible. Tommie and I will handle the rest."

The girl nodded and she and the bat-boy flew off to find other battles to fight.

"Take us down, Tommie," Psy-chick said. "All the way."

The dragon began a long, spiraling descent around Shadow Tower. They were attacked by Shadowmen at every turn. Psy-chick zapped Mordred's minions out of the sky with bolts of lightning while Tommie cleared them from the air with bursts of flame and his long, whipping tail.

At long last, they landed at the base of Shadow Tower. Tommie began to claw his way inside. Hordes of Shadowmen began to descend upon them. Psy-chick blasted away those she could, but there were simply too many.

The Shadowmen gathered along the shore, running into one another until they had joined to form a single, giant mass of ichor. The inky blob shimmered and then shaped itself into a black dragon that was Tommie's equal in every respect. It roared, announcing its intention to attack.

Tommie did not wait on Psy-chick's command to engage the other dragon. He turned and gave his challenger an opposing roar. Psy-chick leaped from Tommie's back just as the two dragons charged each other. They collided and the ground shook beneath their feet.

Their horns locked and they shook their heads back and

forth like warring bucks. They scratched and clawed at each other, tearing away scales and ripping through wing.

The Shadowdragon's one advantage over Tommie was its cold intellect. And it used it to full effect by snaking out its tail between the enraged red dragon's feet, tripping him up. Before Tommie could recover, the Shadowdragon flipped him onto his back, exposing his soft red underbelly.

Psy-chick blasted the Shadowdragon with high intensity volts just as the beast was about to bring down an eviscerating claw.

The Shadowdragon raised its head skyward and howled with pain. Tommie made the most of the distraction and engulfed the black monster in flame. His fire disassembled the dragon into the Shadowmen comprising it. They flew off to look for less challenging opponents.

"Yeah, Tommie!" Psy-chick yelled.

The dragon roared in victory and then licked the length of Psy-chick's body in a single stroke of his giant, pink tongue.

"Oo!" she said. "Now I smell like a chimney. Well, come on, boy! Let's get inside!"

Tommie roared and resumed clawing at the outer wall of Shadow Tower. Within minutes, he'd torn a hole in its side large enough for them to pass through.

Psy-chick climbed onto the dragon and they flew down the throat of the spiraling staircase leading to Shadow Tower's subterranean levels.

They landed in the large hallway that led to their

destination. Tommie charged toward the room. Psy-chick blasted the few Shadowmen standing in his path.

The dragon burst through the doors, knocking them off their giant hinges.

The gigantic, black heart of Shadow Tower stood before them, pumping rivers of ichor throughout the fortress.

"Burn it, Tommie," Psy-chick said. "Burn it all."

Tommie roared and fire leaped from his throat to engulf Shadow Tower's heart in a raging inferno.

Just then, Mordred's ichorous form dropped through the ceiling and piled on the floor like wet, sliding mud. It transformed into the Chance-husk, though scarred flesh now covered its right eye.

Mordred looked at the burning heart of Shadow Tower—his own burning heart—then to Tommie.

"The dragon," Mordred said as he collapsed to the ground. His voice was full of disbelief. "I never could bend him to my will. How did you master him?"

"Mastering had nothing to do with it," Psy-chick said. "*I befriended him.*"

She shook her head at Mordred in pity.

Mordred looked down and saw fire spark on his chest. Then his entire body spontaneously combusted.

Psy-chick stood there, looking at Mordred's blazing, still form. She felt neither satisfaction nor regret. She simply felt numb.

The room began to shake around them. Tommie roared as pieces of the ceiling rained down on them.

"The Shadow Prince is gone and this place is leaving with

him," Psy-chick said. "Come on, Tommie. Let's get out of here."

Tommie galloped out into the hallway and then took wing. They flew back up the stairwell's throat, Shadow Tower coming down around them.

46

Chance crawled over to where Shocker lay and pulled his friend's upper body onto his lap.

"Way to go, Hicksville," Shocker said. "You did all right."

"Don't try to talk," Chance said. "Just lie still. I'll go get help."

"Your friend is dying, fool!" Dr. Faustoid croaked.

"Shut him up!" Chance commanded.

Ribbit clamped his good hand over Dr. Faustoid's mouth.

"Don't listen to him, Shocker," Chance said. "We'll get you out of this!"

"I'm not worried, Chance," Shocker said. "There's no reason to be. No help is needed."

"You're going to be all right," Chance said.

"Yes," Shocker said. His voice was an awe-filled whisper. "Yes, I am. I'm going to be wonderful."

"Now you're talking," Chance said.

Shocker looked skyward through the ceiling's opening, his eyes full and bright.

"Oh, Chance, you should see this! There are worlds beyond imagining! As many as there are drops of water in the sea!"

"You're going into shock," Chance said. "Try to stay conscious. Focus on my voice."

"Chance!" Iron Maiden's voice called from the doorway. "All the Shadowmen have fled the tower! We've routed . . . Shocker?"

Tears flooded from Iron Maiden's eyes.

"Shocker!"

Iron Maiden ran toward them and then skidded to her knees beside Shocker. She grabbed his face in her hands and leaned down, pressing her forehead against his.

"What have they done to you?" Iron Maiden sobbed.

Shocker slowly lifted his arm and stroked Iron Maiden's cheek.

"Shhh. Don't waste your tears on me now, Red. Not a single one. You hear?"

"But I—" Iron Maiden said. "I—"

Iron Maiden buried her face against Shocker's chest. He gently stroked her long, auburn hair.

Then, unexpectedly, Shocker inhaled and let out a whooping yell.

Iron Maiden raised her head to look at him.

"Oh guys," Shocker said. "I'm riding on a comet's tail through the Andromeda galaxy. Woo, this thing sure can buck!"

"What's he talking about?" Iron Maiden asked.

"He's delirious," Chance said. "And in shock. He doesn't know what he's saying."

At that moment, Space Cadet, Private Justice, Gothika, and Viz came running into the room. Each halted in their tracks as they caught sight of Shocker.

"Shocker?" Space Cadet said. "Is he?"

Chance shook his head and Space Cadet began to cry.

"Stop crying, pud," Shocker said. "And get over here. The rest of you, too."

Space Cadet wiped his face and walked slowly over to Shocker. The others followed.

"Shocker," Chance said, tears forming in his eyes, "please forgive me. This is all my—"

"Now hush that nonsense up, Hicksville. This is much bigger than you or me."

"You hang in there, buddy," Private Justice said. "I'll use Gothika's magic. I'll stop this!"

"Stop it?" Shocker said. "Why on Earth would you want to do that?

"Oh! Now I'm beneath the sea glaciers on Europa. There are narwhals here smarter than any of us! They are magnificent!"

Private Justice and the others gazed at Chance in question. Chance shook his head.

Across the room, Ribbit yelped as Dr. Faustoid bit into the frog-boy's hand. Ribbit jerked away and the cyborg bucked the frog-boy from his back. Dr. Faustoid sprang to his feet and ran out of the room.

"Get him!" Chance said.

The Outlaws leaped to their feet.

"No!" Shocker said. "Leave him be. He has his role to play, just as the rest of us."

The Outlaws returned their attention to Shocker.

"You all are the best friends I've ever had," Shocker said. He reached up and rubbed Iron Maiden's chin between his thumb and forefinger. "And I love each and every one of you."

Iron Maiden took Shocker's hand in hers and cradled it against her neck.

"But hard times lie ahead," Shocker said. "My only regret is that I will not be able to face them alongside you."

Shocker looked around the room, making eye contact with each one of them.

"So stick together. Your friendship is the strongest power you have against those who would seek to tear it down."

Shocker's eyes grew distant once again.

"I just watched a new universe being born," Shocker said. "Amazing!"

The Outlaws gasped and took a step back as Shocker's skin began to glow with white light.

"Do not be afraid," Shocker said. "All is well. I go now to a better place—*to all places*."

Shocker's glow brightened, distorting his features so that one was indistinguishable from the next.

Then abruptly he turned to face Chance.

"Chance!" Shocker said, his voice fading as though he were walking down a long hallway. "Before I go, I must tell you. The Vortex Chamber . . . it scattered my essence across the universe . . . I saw everything . . . was everywhere."

Shocker's glow became a brilliant blaze and the Outlaws had to shield their eyes.

"What, Shocker?" Chance asked. "What is it?"

"Your father," Shocker said, his voice now barely audible, "he's alive, Chance. Your father is alive!"

Shocker's glow flashed, bathing the room in blinding white light. Then he was gone. Only his clothes remained.

Iron Maiden scooped Shocker's leather jacket into her arms. Gothika put her arms around the demigoddess as she began to cry. Chance rocked back on his haunches, dumbstruck.

Ribbit gasped as his wart-covered skin began to lift from him like evaporating water. He stood up straight, his body lengthening and slimming, his arm mending. Within seconds, it was no longer Ribbit standing before the Outlaws, but a tall, bald, blue-skinned boy.

"Vox!" Viz cried. "You've changed back!"

"The Shadow Prince's curse has lifted," Vox said.

Viz ran to her brother and wrapped her arms around him.

But time and space paid them no consideration. Each Outlaw was forced back to his or her senses as the room began to tremble around them.

The Vortex Chamber's walls began to crack and splinter as pieces of the ceiling fell to the floor.

"Outlaws," Chance called as he hopped to his feet, "move out!"

They ran as a single unit out into the hallway and down the winding staircase. Iron Maiden put on Shocker's jacket as she brought up the rear.

Chunks of the wall began to rain down Shadow Tower's shuddering length. The Outlaws yelled in terror as the staircase came loose. It crashed against Shadow Tower's other side so that the Outlaws were left hanging for their lives above the seemingly bottomless chasm of Shadow Tower's throat.

The broken staircase creaked and moaned under their weight, threatening to fall apart at any second.

Iron Maiden screamed as she lost her grip. Chance snagged her with his left arm as she came hurtling by him. He looked on in horror as her added weight began to loosen the grip of his scarred hand on the staircase. Space Cadet caught Chance's wrist just as his captain's hand slipped from the railing.

Shadow Tower gave a final roar of protest as it collapsed into a cloud of dust and rubble. The Outlaws screamed as the staircase dropped and sent them tumbling through the air down the length of Shadow Tower.

As they fell, Chance heard another roar—this one distinctly that of an animal. He looked down to see Psy-chick flying toward them on the back of a great red dragon.

Chance snagged a patch of the dragon's scales as it came within reach. Several other Outlaws did likewise. Those who didn't were plucked from the air by the dragon itself.

The dragon rolled, swooped, and banked as it expertly navigated through the last falling pieces of Shadow Tower to bring them high into the air.

As they flew upward, the last of the moons' shadow fell away from the sun's face. For the first time in centuries, its brilliant light shone all around.

47

Ribbit had been the first to be freed from the Shadow Prince's power. The Shadow Zone itself had quickly followed, changing from the gray, scarred landscape to blue skies and green forests, rendering the dimension's name totally inaccurate.

The legions of Shadowmen came next. They transformed back into the superhumans they'd been before falling under Mordred's sway. Most happily reunited with family and friends without incident, including the parents of Viz and Vox. But many showed themselves to truly be the hardened criminals the Brotherhood believed them to be and had to be taken into custody once again.

At high noon, they held a vigil for Shocker in front of a giant, white obelisk that the gangs had erected within a matter of hours. The superhumans had built the structure as a memorial to Shocker and as a lasting reminder of the sacrifices that must be made to ensure freedom.

Vox opened the service with a song heartbreaking in its beauty. All the gang leaders said a few words in Shocker's honor, calling him names like unifier and liberator. Chance spoke last, unsuccessfully choking back tears through most of his speech.

When he was done, Psy-chick stood and zapped the coals in the gold basin at the obelisk's base, igniting a memorial flame. Then she stretched both her hands toward the heavens and let forth a dazzling display of electricity. Those superhumans who could, joined her, sending their own energy beams skyward in salute.

Later, when it was all over, Chance, Psy-chick, Space Cadet, Iron Maiden, Private Justice, and Gothika held their own private memorial for their fallen friend in a tent pitched specifically for the occasion. They laughed and cried in one another's arms, taking comfort and returning it in kind.

After the worst of their immediate grieving had passed, they gathered in a circle with the exception of Chance and Psy-chick to attempt to return their powers back to their rightful owners.

"I don't know if I can do this, Gothika," Private Justice said.

"Yes you can, PJ," Gothika said. "But don't worry. I will guide you. Here, take my hand. Everyone, hold hands."

The Outlaws obeyed and linked hands.

"All that strength," Space Cadet said as he shook his head. "I'm sure going to miss it!"

"It's for the best," Chance said. He and Psy-chick stood watching just outside the circle. "Trust me on that one."

"OK, PJ," Gothika said, "repeat after me."

"Repeat after me," Private Justice said.

Gothika smiled and shook her head. "Not now, PJ. In a second, when I say the spell."

"Not now, PJ, in a—oh. OK."

Gothika looked up at the group. "On the third time, everyone repeat it along with Justice."

They nodded and Gothika turned her head to look directly into Private Justice's eyes.

"OK, PJ, concentrate."

He nodded and Gothika spoke.

"In this circle all around, let that which was lost now be found."

"In this circle all around, let that which was lost now be found."

Gothika and Justice repeated themselves and on the third time the Outlaws spoke in unison.

"In this circle all around, let that which was lost now be found."

A pulsing glow spread over the Outlaws. It flashed softly several times and then petered out.

"Is that it?" Space Cadet asked.

"It should be," Gothika said.

Private Justice brought his hand up to his face and stared at it intensely. When his fingers elongated before his eyes, he cheered with excitement and relief.

"Thank heaven!" Private Justice said. "I thought I was

never going to be rid of that hippie magic! No offense, Gothika."

Gothika lowered her hands and flowers sprouted from the ground to bloom. "None taken."

Iron Maiden picked up a rock from the ground and crushed it in her hand. Though still teary-eyed, she began to smile.

Space Cadet took off his glasses and massaged the bridge of his nose.

"You OK, SC?" Psy-chick asked.

"E equals MC squared," Space Cadet blurted. "An object in motion tends to stay in motion. The speed of light is approximately one hundred eighty-six thousand two hundred eighty-two point four miles per second." SC sighed in relief. "Yeah, I'm okay."

Chance patted his shoulder. The Outlaws followed Chance outside to join the Morlocks. Chance walked up to Caesar and shook his tiny hand.

"So what now?" Chance asked.

"The truce holds," Caesar said, "for now, at least. Perhaps we can work together and rebuild this world—make it a place that adheres to the Code once again."

"Good man," Chance said.

Chance turned to Viz and her parents. They shared their daughter's blue skin and slim physique.

"We will talk to the Brotherhood's governing board," Chance said, "we will tell them what happened here and how wrong it was. We will get them to grant you amnesty and bring you home. I promise."

"Forgive us if we fail to share your confidence, young one," Viz's father said. He looked at Viz's mother and they traded smiles. "Besides, Earth is no longer where we belong. This is home now."

"Pretty Girl!" Vox said. He and Psy-chick laughed as they embraced.

"You are welcome to come with us, you know," Psy-chick said.

"Thank you, Psy-chick," Vox said as he smiled down at her. "But no. My place is here with my family."

Viz held her hand out and Chance took it. Unexpectedly, she leaned forward and kissed him.

Psy-chick cocked an eyebrow.

"As is mine," Viz said.

Chance looked at Psy-chick and shrugged.

The Outlaws said their final good-byes and then joined Psy-chick on Tommie's enormous scaled back.

"Up, up, and away!" Psy-chick yelled and Tommie sprang into the air. He took his time, making long circling arcs that allowed the Outlaws to take in the scenery for miles around. It was as though the dragon knew this would be his final flight with Psy-chick, and he wanted to make it last as long as possible.

At last, Tommie neared the wormhole still shimmering in the sky. He flew alongside the temporal gash and hovered there.

"Where angels fear to tread!" Private Justice cried and then jumped into the wormhole.

"Catch you guys on the flip side," Gothika said and followed after him.

Iron Maiden stood up and adjusted Shocker's jacket were it sat on her shoulders. She gave the Shadow Zone one last look, smiled, and then disappeared into the wormhole.

"Oh," Space Cadet said as he looked at the gap of air between Tommie's back and the wormhole, "this kind of thing was easier when I could knock down trees with my bare hands." Then he was gone, too.

"You be a good boy, Tommie," Psy-chick said as she scratched the dragon's scales. "I'll be back some day. See if you can't find a nice girl dragon to keep you company in the meantime."

Tommie roared. Psy-chick smiled at Chance.

"Coming?"

"Right behind you."

Psy-chick nodded and then leaped into the wormhole. Chance glanced down at his wounded hand and then gave the Shadow Zone a final look. His gaze moved from the obelisk up to the heavens above.

"Good-bye, my friend. I will remember you always."

The sun in the sky blazed and the leaves on the trees rustled in the wind. Whether or not it was in answer, Chance did not know. But he liked to think so.

Chance turned and left the Shadow Zone.

Acknowledgments

Special thanks to Kathleen Doherty, Peter Miller, Adrianne Rosario, Irene Gallo, and Joy Ang.

Shane Berryhill lives with his wife, Lesley, in Chattanooga, Tennessee. He is the author of *Chance Fortune and the Outlaws*. To learn more about Shane, visit the student and educator friendly www.shaneberryhill.com